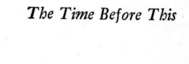

The Time Before This

NICHOLAS

THE
TIME
BEFORE
THIS

MONSARRAT

William Sloane Associates   New York

1962

*

CONTENTS

*

1 BAR ONE

When the old man started shouting, I was standing at the end of the long bar, talking to a couple of construction men and to the bush pilot who had flown me in that morning. We were in the bar of that hotel on Bone Lake, which you will only find on the very latest maps of the Ungava Bay area of Quebec Province. It's the part of Quebec which, with its next-door neighbor Labrador, pushes up into the forlorn frozen wilderness of Hudson Strait. This was all new country, and yet already old—the leapfrog of development which was bursting out all over the Canadian northland had already made it out-of-date.

We were talking about that, and progress, and girls, and my newspaper, and Russia, when the old man went into his act.

I had been watching him out of the corner of my eye for some time, wondering how long they would stand for his particular level of nuisance value. You can always tell, in a bar, when someone is doomed to step out of line, even though you are not involved, and don't intend to be. In this case, I could guarantee from his gaunt anger, his ancient gestures of emphasis, his cracked rising voice, and the smirking of the men nearest to him that the old man would not be with us for very much longer.

They stood for a lot in the bar—which was probably illegal, since they called it a lounge and, for good measure, threw in some nonsense about its being a private club, members only, entrance fee fifty cents. But Bone Lake was a long way from Quebec City and the niceties of the Provincial authority. In fact it was a long way from anywhere; nearer to the Arctic

Circle than I had ever been or (except in the strict line of duty) ever wanted to be.

The bar had all those stage props which are best appreciated on television. The long mahogany counter was backed by rows of bottles with plain or gaudy labels, and then by a flawed mirror which reached to the ceiling. Men came in, stamping the snow and slush off their boots, beating their hands together against the subzero cold. Steam rose from authentic northern clothes: lumberjack shirts, fur caps, checked wind-breakers, coonskin caps—all the romantic trappings which were, in fact, models of utility. It had a piano, untended, and a jukebox, constantly fed with dimes and quarters. But we were not very up-to-date at Bone Lake; the jukebox was playing, for the tenth time since I came in, an ancient close-harmony version of *Lonesome Road*.

There was even a barman called Joe, though one could tell that his name wasn't Joe at all. It was probably Barry, or Earl. But it was part of the canon of conformity hereabouts that all barmen were Joe, just as elsewhere all mayors were corrupt and all mothers sacred. So the customers, playing the same melodrama, hammered on the bar and called out,

"Joe! Hey, Joe! Set 'em up again!" No one was any the worse off for this innocent charade.

Thus it was Joe, a sleek and greasy five-foot-fiver, who was now saying, in a chance moment of silence, "Just simmer down, will you?" And it was the old man who was shouting, on a note suddenly strident:

"I tell you, I *know!*"

What did he *know*, with such Biblical certainty? I turned again to look at him, as did many others. Across the drifts of steam and cigarette smoke, the focus was not sharp; but his face and sometimes his shoulders were in view, above the other people crowding the long bar, because he was a tall old man as well as a noisy one. Yet he was tall like a ruined tower, a gaunt colossus who had ceased to bestride the world; his face had grown pinched and gray, his wispy hair thin, his neck stringy, his shoulders bowed under the weight of the years.

He was an old man who should have been at peace among his grandchildren, and here he was shouting at a bar, beset by a ring of mocking faces.

One could be sorry for him, because the years should have treated him more handsomely. But behavior is what we do, not what is done to us; and he should have known better than to take chances in a world which had passed him by. It was his own fault that he was attracting the mockery of this clan, sticking out his long, stringy neck in order to have it pinched and tweaked. It was his own fault that the reaction was so sharp.

My pilot, whose name was Ed—another authentic piece of characterization—grinned as he nudged me and said:

"The Mad Trapper's acting up again."

I watched, feeling that I should be ashamed, yet feeling only the same kind of idle amusement. My mother, I decided, would have been ashamed for me. . . . The old man had two principal tormentors, who were even now returning to the chase; one was a great beefy fellow, blond, red-faced, sweating under the fur-lined parka which he still wore; the other a small needle-nosed man, a hanger-on, a jackal who would sidle out of the way if the going got rough. Watching, I thought of them as the Ox and the Weasel, and the names will serve.

They had both fallen back a pace when the old man shouted, but now they closed in again, and the Weasel said, sniggering:

"You don't know from nothing, gran'pa. You're for the birds. . . . What is it you know? Tell us what you know."

The old man said, "It's all happened before." His voice was high-pitched, shaking, cutting through the low growl of all the other voices. "We've been here before. That's what I know."

The man I called the Ox pushed an enormous stubby finger into the old man's chest and said, "Is that so? Just prove it, that's all I say. Just prove it."

"I *can* prove it!" shouted the old man. "But not for idiots like you."

"Now just simmer down," said Joe the barman.

"Who are you calling an idiot?" demanded the Weasel. "You want to watch out. My friend here doesn't like to be called an idiot."

"I tell the truth as I see it," said the old man.

"You won't see anything, when I've finished with you," said the Ox. He gave the old man a slow, heavy shove, and he fell back against the bar. "You call me an idiot again, and I'll break you up."

"You pushed me!" screamed the old man. I could not see him now, but his voice—astonished, indignant, slurred by alcohol—weaved through the air between us and found my ear. "You used force! . . . But you cannot silence the truth!"

"I can give it a damn good try," said the Ox, and shoved again, viciously, at the gaunt body which still remained out of my line of sight.

"Simmer down, now," said Joe.

The old man bobbed into view again, his arms flailing wildly. "Don't touch me!" he shouted. "You —you animal!"

Other voices now began to rise, protesting—but they were protesting their own discomfort, not the old man's indignity. "Pipe down!" "I came here to enjoy myself!" "Break it up!" "Give us a rest!" —the chorus of disapproval made itself heard throughout the room. Some of the card players turned from their tables, and one of them called out, "Hey, Joe! We're trying to concentrate. Make him shut up." Unfairly, inevitably, the tide was turning against the old man. I did not think he would be staying with us much longer.

Then I noticed the girl—or rather, I re-noticed her, because I had taken a brief look at her earlier. She was not too young, not too pretty, not too alluring; she was a girl on a stool at a bar. I don't like girls on bar stools, though I'm not making an issue out of it; if they want to wait there, let them wait there—as long as I don't have to be a customer. *Look down, look down, that lonesome road*, the jukebox had been moaning when I first saw her; and I had thought, without too big a catch in my throat, how lonesome that road must be, how joyless, how not for me.

She had been sitting on her stool, watching, killing time, sipping economically, smiling the mirthless smile of girls in bars. But now, astonishingly, she stepped down, and went forward, and said to the Ox:

"Why don't you leave him alone?"

It was as if a cut-out paper doll had suddenly complained about the scissors. The big man turned, as surprised as I had been. "What the hell?" he said, almost stammering. "And what's it to you?"

"He's not doing any harm," said the girl. She was small, and thin rather than slim; her back was towards me, but the set of her head was determined. "Why don't you pick on someone your own weight?"

It might have become interesting; but, as it happened, that was the last I heard of the exchange. Suddenly the quarrel grew private; attention shifted, voices rose elsewhere, the temperature dropped perceptibly. I could see the Ox man and the girl arguing, but their voices were lower, their expressions less sullen and significant. The heat seemed to be off. I turned back to Ed the pilot.

"What's this?" I asked. "Who's the old nuisance?"

Ed grinned again, swirling the drink round in his glass. "They call him the Mad Trapper—among other things. He's always doing this. I think his name is Shepherd. Same routine every night. He starts an argument, then someone gets fed up and he's thrown out."

"What sort of argument?"

"Strictly the rye-and-water kind," answered Ed. "There's no sense in any of it. . . . He always says, 'It's happened before.' Then he says, 'I *know!*' " He was mimicking the old man's anguished tones with a certain skill. "He's a regular feature around here."

"But what does he *do?*"

Ed shrugged. "Gets drunk. Gets into arguments. Gets thrown out. End of story." He turned back to the bar, prepared to forget it. "What time do you want to take off tomorrow?—*if* we can take off."

We talked and made some tentative plans, depending on tomorrow's cold, and the chance of fog, and the time it might take to blowtorch a frozen engine into life. But my interest in the old man had not died so quickly. I was still wondering what it was all about, what could have moved him to such torment, such distraught violence. Maybe, as Ed said, it was just the bottle—in which case there was no story for me there. None, indeed. I hadn't come these many miles to write about old drunks in bars; I could do that at home, any time, any day. A drunk is a drunk is a drunk, in Toronto or Tahiti. My hoped-for target was something better.

But I was not quite finished with the old man for that night; his ability to disturb and annoy was persistent, and in the end it included me. His voice, freshly raised, now made itself heard again. I looked up, to see him staggering sideways away from the bar. The girl was pulling at one arm, and he was brandishing the other one and shouting:

"I have proof! Positive proof!"

"Here we go again," said Ed.

"Simmer down," said Joe the barman. "Or you'll have to leave."

"Come on," said the girl, pulling at his arm again. "I'll take you home."

"You take him home," said the Weasel, baring his teeth unpleasantly. "And the best of luck to you."

But the Ox, his overlord, was less accommodating. "You take him home," he threatened, "before I take him apart."

The old man suddenly drew himself up. "You are a barbarian," he said very clearly, with tremendous authority. Then, just as suddenly, he seemed to suffer a collapse of spirit; defiance faded into a trembling fatigue; one could divine now that the tall body was as gaunt and frail as the face. Shambling, flapping his arms, he allowed the girl to lead him towards the doorway.

They passed close by us. I found myself watching the girl, wondering about her motives, wondering why, of all people, she had been the only one to take the old man's side. Maybe he had some money left. . . . I found that I could not extend her much credit, nor belief; harlots with hearts of gold were only good enough for Broadway; hard fact inevitably proved them to be selfish, greedy, and corrupt in all things. What else could they be?

The old man's eyes were closed as he shuffled by; the girl might have been leading a blind cripple. But when he reached the door, his voice rose on a final burst of energy.

"It has all happened before!" he shouted over his shoulder. Then the door swung outwards, and the strange pair were gone, with the girl serving as a crutch under his elbow. One had to admit that she was the only one to come out of this with any sort of a plus sign. I hoped it would be worth her trouble.

"It's all happened before, to *him*," said Ed with a laugh. "And that's for sure."

"Who's the girl?"

"Called Mary. Mary, Mary, not too contrary."

Lonesome Road had started up again. *Look up, look up, and seek your Maker*, sang the jukebox. I felt ill at ease, for no known reason; the incident, which should have been funny, was now merely pitiful. I was sorry that I had laughed—that any of us had laughed. Old men, however foolish or crazed, deserved something better than laughter at the end of their own long lonesome road.

"Now we can all simmer down," said Joe the barman, appearing suddenly in front of us, perky as a canary. "What's it to be?"

"Nothing for me," I said. "Early start. . . . I see you just lost a good customer."

"Oh, him." Joe, swabbing down the bar, sniffed his disdain. "He's just a nut. Though to hear him tell it, he's the only one in the whole wide world who isn't."

＊

2 I WAS THERE

For at least three weeks I forgot the old man, and the girl Mary, and their off-beat exit from the bar at Bone Lake. I had work to do, work which grew steadily more fascinating. I was there in the northland because I had been sent there, by an editor who dispatched us lesser mortals to our deaths in tropical hurricanes or to a yawning doom at local council meetings with an equal zest. Bill Bradman had been my taskmaster on

the Toronto *Journal* for five years; he was just beginning, very slowly, very grudgingly, to admit that,
given help, advice, a series of recurrent jolts, and lavish
slashings of his blue pencil, I could occasionally be
trusted to turn in a story which presented certain
shadowy aspects of the printed truth.

This northland assignment was my first big one. I
had started out by thinking that I could whistle my
way through it with a typewriter, two fingers, and a
little leg work. I came swiftly to realize that the assignment, like the north, was really big.

What I had in mind—no, even that is an exaggera-
tion—what Bradman had in *his* mind, and had therefore implanted in mine, was a series of articles which
would bypass the customary romantic, frozen-North
nonsense and present the Canadian northland in its
true aspect, which was industrial pioneering on a gi-
gantic scale. ("None of your Mountie-bank stuff,"
Bradman had cautioned me, with a grin which
changed to a glare when he saw that I had got the
joke.) For nearly two centuries North America had
been discovered, opened up, planted and peopled on a
roaring axis which ran from east to west. Now the
compass had swung, and the long legs of progress

were striding northwards on a brand-new trail. I wanted to find out, and to tell, what that trail was like. I wanted to tell it, in the first place, to Canadians, because by and large we know as little about its real pattern as do the Formosan Chinese.

Bone Lake was a jumping-off point, for the pioneering process as well as for myself. The very town itself had been dropped from the air, brought in piece by piece, in a fantastic series of helicopter lifts, together with the cement, the steel, the cranes, and the men to bolt it all together.

It had been built, populated, and lived in, all within six months. Grocery bills were being paid, or not paid, long before the last hammer stroke faded on the brittle air; love was made there before the first railway tie was even hewn. It was part of the fabulous leap-frog of this century; first the town was flown in, then the rail link snaked northwards to join it. Later there might be a road, if the road, like the railway, could be made to float on top of a semiliquid, semi-frozen peat bog, five hundred miles from end to end.

But already Bone Lake was the springboard for the next jump ahead; already, only three years old, it was an old-fashioned town, serving a frontier which had

already been pushed northwards over a hundred glacial hills; already it was in decay. It was like a Western
cowboy town, but frozen stiff in restless history; built
on stilts above the permafrost—the icy slush which
served for ground hereabouts—it seemed doomed to
inherit, within a decade, the moldering graveclothes
of Klondike and Dawson City.

As in so many other parts of Canada, the rule was
boom or bust, feast or famine; it was chicken one day,
feathers the next. For Bone Lake, now a mere way-
station on the road to the bounding future, it would
soon be feathers again.

Not all its transients could save it—its survey teams,
its replacements for the Dew Line crews and for the
American bomber stations. Not all its brash fortune
hunters, its spongers and drifters, its people like me;
nor its lost-looking Eskimos and its tribal aristocrats—
the Indians working on the high steel. Not all this restless tide of toughs and tradespeople and friendly
finance men could keep it alive for very much longer.

Except for an ex-king, there could be nothing so *ex*
as an ex-frontier; and this was ordained as Bone Lake's
doom. Once more, new life lay to the north and
northwest, opening up in a giant sky-wide fan like

the glittering northern lights themselves. It was there that men were staring, and heading, and hurrying, as fast as people like Ed the pilot could carry them. Casualties such as Bone Lake could only be left behind, bobbing and sinking in the wake of the advance.

I came to know those northern lights very well on my crisscross journeys around and about the Arctic Circle. They were beautiful, like the banners of hope; white and pale yellow and ghostly blue, flickering and fading, filling the whole night sky like a Christmas candle-glow ten thousand miles across. Reflections from far northern ice, they tell us, or cloud layers moving, or vapor trails which mirrored a midnight sun. But in Greenland they are *known* to be the souls of the dead playing ball with the skulls of seals. This is much the best explanation I ever heard.

I came to know Ed very well also, and to like him. He was a type, but an essential and admirable one, and as much a part of the northland scene as the waste of snow itself. In a quarter-century of flying, he and his fellow pilots had had a notable share in the opening up of the new frontier. Without Ed and about fifty men like him, the Canadian north would still be lagging.

Ed had flown everywhere, from Baffin Island to

Alaska and the far west; he had carried men and dogs and stores and machine tools; he had crashed gently into half-frozen lakes, and taken off blind into swirling snow blizzards. He knew it all, and what he knew was still only just enough, as he admitted, to keep him and his plane in one piece.

With me, he answered questions when they were asked, and his answers were accurate and revealing, filling out the thousand silly gaps in my knowledge. But basically he was a non-talker; when he was on the job he fell into a dedicated trance; he would sit stock-still in enormous concentration, as if ready to lift the plane and keep it aloft by its own stirrups.

Sometimes he paid no attention to me at all, and he would explain, ten minutes later, that something had been "a tricky bit." Once he said curtly, "Shut up a minute," and when next I glanced aside we were banking sharply, and climbing steeply, and still looking *up* at a craggy, pitted iceberg which had loomed out of the low-lying fog like a suddenly raised fist.

When we had emerged, and I was still sweating, he said, "Sorry." I realized he meant that he was sorry to have shut me up. But I was far from objecting. As long as he worried, I knew I did not have to.

Ed planned all our journeys, knowing what I wanted to see and, more important still, what other things I must not miss. It was a harsh and desolate land, but wildly beautiful; if, as the history books say, Jacques Cartier called it "the land God gave to Cain," then Cain did much better than he deserved. Of course, there were places like the Hudson Strait, fog-shrouded and raw, which were indeed forbidding; the miles of glacial tundra were as ugly as all featureless things must be; and there were other ominous wastes of ice and snow, tormented by cruel weather, where the price of laggard traveling would certainly be death.

But against the grim and the ravaged, there were four attributes which constantly recurred on all our voyaging. They were beauty, nobility, human kindness, and hope. On balance, this northland was no frozen wilderness. Under its austere fabric was a warm and beating heart; under the battleground, the good earth of valor and love.

We had so many cordial welcomes that I lost count of names and places. For the most part it must have been due to Ed, a popular and even famous character who was greeted everywhere with an invariable,

open-handed pleasure. He was their link with the outside, the tested link which they had come to trust in
sickness, in evil times, in disaster. At one little hamlet
near Frobisher, they knew him as "the Mercy Man";
the label bespoke the lore of some memorable rescue
a dozen years earlier. But I had the feeling that if I,
alone and a stranger, had dropped in upon any of these
isolated settlements, I would have been made to feel
just as much a friend.

It was something—it was really something—to fly
for two or three hours in a bucking, not too warm, not
too comfortable plane across an ancient spreading icecap known to be two miles thick, or a wasteland inhabited only by ghostly gray wolves and wandering
caribou and the musk oxen which looked like the
world's shaggiest dogs, and then to set down at a trad-
ing post or a hamlet where the sound of our plane
brought men and children running, and where we
stepped out into a ring of smiling, welcoming faces.

The pattern was always the same; it warmed the
heart with the same eye-pricking suddenness every
time. Foremost in the reception committee would be
the three wise men of all these communities—the
trader, the priest, and the policeman. Behind them was

this circle of beaming Eskimos—the bundled-up, indistinguishable men and women, the rolypoly children, the dogs on holiday from their snarling; and behind them again the tiny village of tar-paper houses and corrugated iron shacks, made to seem more wretched still by the brief, revealing midday sun. But they only *seemed* wretched. The shacks and the sheds and the half-buried igloos were home town, and we were as welcome there as flowers at midsummer. The smiling faces told us that, on every occasion.

"I don't know what they've got to smile about," said Ed once. "They have *nothing!* If a man loses a single harpoon in winter, ten people can starve to death. And why smile at *us?* By and large, we hardly do a damn thing for them. Not what we should. Not what we *could.* But they always smile. They smile when you tell them they're dying of T.B. They must be the last of the naturally happy people. Or else resigned to it." He sighed. "Sometimes it makes you ashamed to own a ten-dollar bill."

I was sure that, of all people, he need feel the least ashamed; and he must in fact have come to realize this himself. Our welcome was always real, beyond belief; the night-long gossip, the laughter, the hallowed practical jokes, the broad pantomime—all bore witness to an unalterable friendship. When we took our leave, even at such a horrid hour as five o'clock in the morning, the good-byes were always a community affair, boisterous and true. Though their friend was leaving, they trusted him to come back again.

These were the simple places. There were others, larger, more sophisticated, which could boast a mayor, a chamber of commerce, a Rotarian glad hand. Their hospitality was perhaps a calculated matter; a traveling newspaperman might sanctify their names in print. But all was forgivable when measured against the hard work they were doing. The pioneers of this thriving wilderness must be allowed their share of the limelight, since they had sparked the light themselves.

There were other places, sophisticated in a grisly sense, places which I disliked by instinct while admitting that the twentieth century gave them some kind of sanction. We would follow a meandering ore train across Labrador, and lose it, and fly over icy seas, and snow slopes, and the great nothingness of the northland; and then our next landfall would be a cluster of radar domes, and U.S. army hutments, and enormous supply depots, and snowmobiles instead of dog sleds, and an underground life as complex and metropolitan as New York. These were the men on guard, the men on the far side of the Arctic medal; watchmen on the special sectors of the Dew Line, surrounded by the fearful toys manufactured for an age of fear.

They were cheerful men, but preoccupied, aloof. While we were casual visitors, they were the steadfast garrison. We dropped in, they stayed put. When asked for details, they grew cagey, turning questions into woolly answers, and answers into jokes. Under their standing orders, they had no other choice save this frivolity. But it was sad to realize that soldiers in this majesty and splendor of the north must look further north again, and discover only enemy masks.

Yet while men could adorn or deface the great canvas, it remained a sublime masterpiece. For me, all its magic could be summed up in one single scene, observed on the last day of our tour, when we flew eastwards from Pond Inlet, and down the length of Baffin Island, and then back to our home base on Bone Lake. Over Baffin, whose seaboard rises in great, steep-to, three-thousand-feet cliffs to a tremendous spine of icy mountains, we came upon the ultimate in Arctic splendor.

It stood at the end of an enormous, hidden, un-ruffled fjord; it could only be called an ice castle. Its peak must have been over six thousand feet high, reaching imperiously for the sun; its base was pure blue ice, falling headlong into the sea. In between, it rose tier upon tier in the fantastic architecture of raw nature; if ten million years had gone to the making of this sculptured fortress, not one of them had been wasted.

I gazed at it in entrancement while Ed, without any prompting, made a second pass over it, and then a third. When he saw my face, he smiled and nodded downwards in agreement. He was not the man to be awed even by this magnificence, but he was a man to be confident in the wares he could set before me.

While we were droning our way southwards again, on the last lap of our journey, I said:

"You kept the best till the last."

He looked up from his instrument panel, his hands steady and relaxed on the controls. "It's quite some-thing, isn't it? . . . There are two or three like that. . . . No one knows anything about them, except that they're *there*."

"What's underneath it?"

"Ice. Then rock. Then God knows what." The plane wavered slightly in a drift of vapor, and he bore down with a controlling hand. "This is a funny part of the world. You get things like that mountain of ice, which should have eroded away long ago. And they've found whales' skeletons a thousand feet above high-water mark."

I said, "You'll have to translate for me."

Ed grinned. "Well, whales can't fly. Never could. The old sea level must have been that much higher."

"When?"

"At the beginning. When the first ice was melting. It was a kind of colossal spring runoff. But this was the very spring of the world."

The very spring of the world. . . . The poetic phrase, so odd-sounding on the lips of this gruff, monosyllabic man, stayed with me on all our homeward journey. The ice castle stayed with me also, noble and memorable, never fading from the inward eye. Its towering might had seemed to crown the whole northland.

It was from such majestic prospects that I returned to Bone Lake, to watch once again the old man at the bar making an arrant fool of himself.

3 BAR TWO

I had planned to write the core of my story there at Bone Lake, while it was fresh in my mind and the atmosphere itself was still available to help me; then travel a bit more to pick up the loose ends; then go back home to tie the whole thing up in a good solid knot. But the writing was slow because I wanted it to be good—good enough to match the country; and on the third day, only halfway through, I pushed back my chair, and stretched, and shaved, and wandered down to the hotel bar in search of company.

I felt I needed to take a breather, and to look at something else besides a typewriter keyboard and a dreary, hollow hotel room.

The company was there. It was the same company as before, and the same interior scene, and the same cast of leading characters. But this time they were playing it harder. And this time I was close by.

The thin girl called Mary sat on her stool, watching, waiting. Joe the barman bobbed about, dispensing good fellowship at sixty cents a pledge. Ed bought me a drink. The Ox man and the Weasel man, now at my end of the bar, began walking through their crude roles. Their victim began his same act in the same doomed way.

This time he was giving us a longer monologue: full of wild and whirling words, recalling an old-time preacher who could only hope to hold his audience by noisy melodrama. I caught snatches of it. The phrase "I *know!*" was always there, like some idiotic sales slogan. And something about the time before this. And something about punishment, and something about our last chance, and total destruction, and human survival. It made as much sense as before, and that could not be construed as a compliment.

Yet he did not deserve the rough treatment they handed him. There were more charitable ways of dealing with an old eccentric than by baiting him to distraction. And if charity was not the long suit at Bone Lake, as at any other place, then practicality might have taken its place. An old man out of his wits could hardly be an asset to the gathering.

Or so I thought. But I realized that I might be one of a naïve minority as I watched the ring of faces around the old man—a smiling ring, though not at all like the Eskimos—and heard the undertone of taunting comment. The silly old man was their first choice of fun. The conviction became stronger still as the Weasel, with an atrocious public wink, minced up to him and said:

"You had another vision, Pop? Tell us about it. Or would you rather pass a miracle?"

In the laughter, the old man's reply was lost. But it seemed that he was now struggling for self-control; the furious face, seamed with age, yellow-white beneath the smoky lamplight, was working and trembling under the pressure of some inner mastery. When silence fell, the Weasel asked:

"What was that again, Pop? We missed that pearl."

With threadbare dignity, the old man took a slow sip of his drink, staring at the Weasel over the rim of his glass. Then he set it down on the counter, and turned back, and answered:

"I said, do not address me as Pop."

The Weasel sniggered. "What's your name then, Pop?"

"You know my name well enough. I am Mr. Shepherd."

"No kidding. . . ." The Weasel, not liking the change of pace, sought about for a new probe. But he was forestalled by his friend, the man I called the Ox. The Ox, who had been following the exchange in silence, was now gesturing for attention with a sweep of his arm; his mouth was opening and closing, on the verge of some notable contribution. The Weasel chipped in. "Silence for my friend!" he called. "My friend has something to say."

The Ox raised a stubby forefinger and tapped the old man on the chest. He spoke with tremendous self-conceit, as if he knew he had the best line in the play.

"What I want to know," he said. "If you're a shepherd, where's your sheep?"

After the build-up, it was so ludicrous that it won a roar of laughter. Some of the card players turned to join in. I even grinned myself. I had forgotten the old man's name was Shepherd. For a moment it seemed to add the final touch to a foolish fantasy in which an ox asked an acute question and a shepherd lost his flock. For a moment it seemed that the old man deserved all he got, including our laughter.

But only for a moment. The Weasel, giggling, said, "That's a good one! That's the best crack I ever heard!" The Ox smirked round about him in triumph. The old man, embattled and mocked, turned away, shaking his head, blinking up at the light, silenced by inanity. I knew then that I should not even have grinned.

To cover shame and irritation, I turned away myself and spoke to Ed. I said the first thing that came into my mind, reverting to something we had been talking about earlier.

"At the present rate, another fifty years will see the whole northland opened up. It's a fantastic prospect!"

My voice must have been sharp, to emphasize a change of subject; and I was unlucky to hit a moment of silence. A few people looked towards me, as men do when they hear a new voice. But it was the old man himself who whipped around, and glared directly into my face, and shouted:

"It is not fantastic at all! It is normal! It is history!"

Suddenly everyone was looking at me. The girl swung round from the bar counter, on guard for my reaction; her face seemed smaller, pinched by anxiety that she might have yet another rescue on her hands. The Weasel watched me closely, needing to know if I were an ally or an enemy. The Ox stared at me, discovered that I was younger and smaller, and wrote me off with a contemptuous jerk of the head. Other people at the bar glanced from the old man to me, sizing up the match. Even Joe the barman moved a few steps in my direction and muttered, "Simmer down, now," as if he feared a new focus of discord. In the space of a few seconds I had become part of the show.

It was not at all what I wanted. If anything, I sided with the old man, the forlorn underdog; I certainly did not want to argue with him, nor join the yapping majority. But apart from that, barroom brawls were not to my taste in any case. Leading nowhere, they wasted boundless energy on the way; they shared a bracket with casual love and greedy politics as the worst of adult play areas. And if that sounds priggish, I claim to belong to a generation whose elders drink too much, think too little, tell too many lies, strike too many attitudes, abdicate too freely and too soon. That doesn't leave very much to us children except the resulting problems, which are not our own, and the priggishness, which is.

Given these stray thoughts within this solemn frame of reference, I could only do my best not to get involved; I could only play it light. Thus I met the old man's eye, squarely enough for honesty, and said:

"O.K. So it's normal. I'm not arguing."

But I had played it too light; he must have thought that I was writing him off as a negligible nuisance (which perhaps was true), and his reaction was fierce, almost hysterically so. He gave me a look of absolute resentment, which clearly classed me with the rest of the enemy world, and said in a shrill voice:

"You're not arguing because you cannot argue!

You talk of opening up the northland as if it had some special virtue, as if it had just been invented. But it is nothing! It has all been done before. I can prove it."

This didn't make any sense at all, but, once again, I was determined to avoid the battle. If he had some crackpot theory about the North, he was welcome to it. I made as if to turn back to my drink, and answered offhand:

"If you can prove it, then good luck to you."

But my disengagement was not working out at all well. "You don't believe me!" he screamed. "Your manner is insolent!" He advanced a step towards me, shaking his fist, nearly dancing with rage. "You are like the rest of them, ignorant and stupid. You young puppy!"

His antics had already brought back the corporate mockery of the barroom; now the absurd word *puppy*, mouthed with such authority—as if it were the most hurtful in the whole calendar of invective—set off a wild disturbance. It was the Weasel who started it; as soon as he heard the word he threw back his head and called, "Woof, woof!" on a high-pitched, whining note. Suddenly everyone began to copy him; the whole room resounded to an animal clamor, a horrible rise and fall of barkings, growlings, yappings, howling catcalls.

It was as if we had all decided, in a single moment of degradation, to take a step backwards into a wolfish world, the kingdom of the zoo. A few men, perfectionists, capered about on all fours. One of them rolled over on his back, puppy paws in the air, as if begging forgiveness for all our sins.

The old man, utterly taken aback by the insane uproar, stood mute. When I looked towards him, I found that I was meeting his eyes; when I glanced sideways, I met the girl's eyes instead. They bore the same message—that it was I who had brought on this uproar, that it was all my fault. For a moment I had hoped that the barking and the foolishness would blank out my own part in this and let me off the hook. Now, meeting those lingering eyes, I was not sure that I was free.

The noise subsided gradually; men, cackling with laughter at their own buffoonery, drew in to the bar again and ordered fresh drinks to celebrate. But there was one man, slow of wit, who was still unappeased; he was still there, a monument to dogged ill will, and he still wanted the floor.

It was the Ox. He stood immovable by the bar, facing the old man, scowling. Finally he said, in direct threat:

"You haven't answered my question."

"Question?" The old man turned. He was a different old man already; tired, dispirited, shocked by the few mindless moments of chaos. "What question?"

"You know damn well what question. . . . If your name's Shepherd—remember?"

"I don't understand you."

"If your name's Shepherd, where's your sheep?"

It had sounded mildly funny before; now it had taken a turn into menace, into lunacy. The old man faced his tormentor, shaking his head, uncomprehending; it was clear that he really did not understand. At last he said:

"There is some confusion here. . . . That is not what we were discussing."

" 'That is not what we were discussing,' " repeated the Ox in ferocious mimicry. He advanced a step nearer, till he loomed over the old man like a darkening cliff. "O.K., Pop—what were we discussing?"

There was complete silence around them now. By my side Ed murmured, as he had done before, "Here we go again." But it was on a different note this time, a note of pity and doom. I saw to my discomfort that, while everyone nearby was watching the old man, the girl Mary was watching me.

The old man rallied, with a last spark of pride. "We were discussing the northland. I maintain this is not the first time it has been inhabited on a high level of development. In fact, I can prove it."

"Go ahead and prove it," said the Ox. "I've got time."

"This is not the moment." He faced the Ox bravely. "And you are not the man."

"Is that so?" The Ox reached out and grasped the old man by the lapels of his coat. A buttonhole ripped under the ferocious grip. "You go ahead and prove it. Like I said."

Out of the corner of my eye I saw the girl getting down off her stool. But, to my own amazement, I was on the move also, ahead of her. For no reason in the world I was walking into this, to help an old fool from the clutches of a brute. For no reason I suddenly felt that I owed the old man a rescue. Only God knew why.

Still a few steps away, I called out, "Give him a rest."

The Ox, tall enough to see me over the old man's shoulder, focused his gaze and found me. I was sweating, but the next few moments were something I had to go through.

The Ox said, "You talking to me?"

It was a rhetorical question, and I remembered the rules of grammar. "You've had your fun. . . . Just let him go."

"Who's going to make me?"

"No one's going to make you. But I think he's had enough."

Behind me there was a movement, and then Ed's voice, "That goes for me, too."

From round about us there came a curious throaty murmur, difficult to define; to my lonely heart it sounded like a late-stirring sympathy. On the face of the Ox, broad puzzlement showed. I was small. Ed was large. It was not clear how many allies we had, but probably, in reaction, we had some. The Ox hesitated, and then he growled, "Arrh—the hell with it!" and let go his grip, and turned, to us and to the world, his enormous back.

As the old man staggered away, Mary neatly caught his arm and twisted him towards the door. Then they walked out together, without a sound or a pause.

Joe the barman was the first to break the silence, with the last word from authority. In a little snarly voice he called out to the empty, swinging doorway:

"Next time, the police!"

*

4 MARY MOTHER OF NOTHING

I watched the northern lights for a long, long hour after I got back to my room. They were clean and white on that night; they moved very slowly, giving a steadfast beauty to the crisp, cold sky. Watching them across a range of glistening roof tops, I felt more than ever that they looked down on worthless men. The sum of foolishness, cruelty, and cowardice which had made up our contribution that evening could not deserve such riches.

Not at all in the mood for work, I was taking these sad thoughts to bed when there was a knock on my door, and Mary walked in.

I was not ready for her; not in mood, not in dress, not in inclination. But she must have walked into many rooms, wanted or not wanted, unannounced or heralded by song; the entrance was precise, self-assured, a statement of policy rather than a question mark. Once she was inside, the door swung shut behind her as if part of some confederate act. Then she smiled briefly and briskly, and said:

"Hi!"

I was barefooted and taking off my tie; she had me at a disadvantage, in a pattern I did not like. Close to —and by now she *was* close to, crossing the room in quick, clicking steps—she was just as I expected; she had the fatal air of having been mauled by men, of being the end product of careless or brutal use. Good manners, and tolerance as well, evaporated as I said:

"What do you want?"

She must have heard that kind of greeting, also,

many times; it did not check her. Without a change of expression she answered:

"I wanted to say thanks for what you did tonight."

"That's O.K." Though the excuse was reasonable enough, I was wary still; in this particular area, one thing led to another, and I did not want to trigger any of it. "I thought the old man was getting a rough deal."

"He always does."

"But it's his own fault."

"Oh sure, sure."

The disbelieving tone was just enough to needle me. Unwisely, I tried to make my point.

"Well, it *is* his own fault. If liquor hits him that hard, he should stay out of bars."

"Lots of people should stay out of bars."

Silence fell again. She was looking around the room, taking in the snow clothes, the typewriter, the serviceable luggage. She was painfully thin; the face, which properly fleshed might have been beautiful, was positively skull-like. What she needed, I thought, was a solid program of steak dinners. But I wasn't in the steak-dinner business, and I wasn't going to be.

She said, "You're a writer, aren't you?"

"Newsman."

There was a bottle of whisky on the night table. I saw her looking at it, but I wasn't going to trigger that sequence, either. I went on unknotting my tie. Finally she said:

"Well, like I said, I just wanted to thank you."

"Forget it."

"Ed was a real help, too."

"He's a good man."

She looked at me directly and steadily for the first time. "So are you," she said. Then, as if to show that she could match me on any ground, that she had pride to wear as well as clothes, she nodded, and turned, and was gone.

Her footsteps receding down the bare corridor were businesslike, unhesitating. They conveyed the clear message that she wouldn't have come back for at least a hundred dollars.

She came back next day, for nothing, because I asked her to. There were various reasons for this turn-about, which on the face of it was stupid. Primarily, I had a bad conscience; I knew that, in a better mood, I would at least have acknowledged her effort to thank me. I didn't want to get involved, but, equally, I didn't have to be rough about it—or so it appeared by the more liberal light of day.

Then, I was bored. The northland story was only limping from my typewriter, because I kept feeling that there must be much more to it than I had found out. Or a better story hiding somewhere—something like that. That was not the climate for writing—it was the climate for making excuses and doing something else instead. The choice of something else, in Bone Lake, was not wide. Talking to Mary was a ready-to-hand alternative.

Finally, she had intrigued me—not as a person, but as an element in a situation. I wanted to know about her and the old man; why she was involved, and what she was involved in. I wanted to know more about him, and for this she was the best lead.

For these reasons—if they were the reasons—I smiled when I met her in the lobby next day. Then I said, "I owe you a drink," and she nodded, as if we were continuing a conversation, and answered, "Twelve o'clock."

We talked all afternoon, up in my room, with sandwiches to help out, and a bottle to help me. She had brought, of all things, her knitting—it was a scarf for the old man—and she sat on the shabby sofa by the window, her hands busy, her eyes intent on her work, her voice making a thread of the facts, like the yellow wool she worked with. It was a good voice, full, deep, belying her thin face and meager body; it was a voice not ashamed of emotion, nor ashamed of silence if silence would serve the story.

More than once she asked me if I wanted to work. The answer was always no.

Because I was inquisitive, our talk was, to begin with, mostly about her. Like the majority of men, I knew more about her by hearsay than by experience. Prepared for excuses, for a romantic gloss on a coarse fabric, I was surprised by the austerity of fact. Many hallowed superstitions went by the board as I listened to her answers.

She was not a clergyman's daughter orphaned at sixteen. She was not a stranded chorus girl working off her hotel bill. She was not a widow with a tiny pension and two piteous mouths to feed. She had not fled from a Peeping-Tom stepfather. She had not been seduced by this rich politician's son and run out of town by the chief of police.

She was a working girl, like her mother before her. She had come to Bone Lake because Montreal was too tough. She did not especially like her job, but she did not like any other job better.

She was thus an honest woman, and many of her thoughts were immaculate. Particularly where they concerned the old man. We had talked about the number of times she had come to his rescue, and I had wondered, out loud, why.

"He needs help," she answered flatly, as I seemed ready to dismiss him as a nuisance. "People should help each other."

"But what's his trouble?"

"Booze. And some funny ideas that may be right and may be wrong. And he's old and sick as well."

"Then he should see a doctor."

She said, with finality, "He's seen one."

"Oh. . . . Then he shouldn't be getting into these rows."

"That's something he feels he must do." She looked at me and then down to her knitting again. She produced, from her compassionate storehouse, another maxim. "People should be sorry for other people."

"But he's just a drunk."

"Who isn't?"

"Don't say that! You know it's not true."

"All right—" she smiled at my vehemence—"I mean, who *doesn't* have some kind of a weakness?"

"But you're supposed to fight it. . . . So all this means that you're sorry for him."

"Just that." She looked at me again, more defiantly, daring me to suggest otherwise. "He doesn't have any money."

I think that was the moment, sometime during the late afternoon, when the bottle ebbed, things warmed up, and I made a conventional attempt to kiss her. But all she said was, "You don't really want to," and we left it like that, without embarrassment, and went back to what we had been talking about, which was now exclusively the old man.

"How long have you known him?"

"Two years," she answered. "Since I've been here."

"You know they call him the Mad Trapper?"

"They always call someone the Mad Trapper. That's standard hereabouts."

"What about these funny ideas he has?" And as she did not answer, I pursued it. "He's always saying, 'I *know*,' at the top of his voice. What does he know?"

Her face was averted, not giving much away. "It's something he's found. Or thinks he's found."

"Thinks?"

"Well, it's hard to believe."

"But you believe it?"

Now her head came up, and her hands were still. "Yes, I believe it."

"But what is it?"

"I can't tell you."

"What sort of thing?"

"I can't tell you," she repeated. "I promised not to."

"Who else has he told?"

This was something she was definite about. "Over the years, he's told seven people."

"And?"

"They think he's round the bend. But they're wrong!"

"That all depends. What sort of people were they?"

Her head came up again, with an odd kind of pride. She recited, as if from some well-learned text, "The Pope. President Truman. The Archbishop of Canterbury. Nehru. Stalin. Mr. St. Laurent when he was prime minister here. And some English king."

I looked at her sharply, wondering if she had started to play the fool. But her face was quite serious.

"You mean, he went to see all those people?"

"No. He wrote to them."

"Oh." The picture was becoming clearer, and more conventional. There were people who wrote letters to popes and prime ministers and kings, and other people who did not. The dividing line was usually clear. "You said, an English *king*. Then this was some time ago."

"About twenty years. Maybe more. He tried to go back—" She stopped suddenly and put her hand over her mouth in the schoolgirl gesture of dismay. She had said too much, perhaps by a single word, and I jumped on it.

"Then it was some place he found? Or some man?"

She shook her head, refusing to answer. But I wasn't going to be put off; the process of deduction was too tempting.

"If he *tried* to go back and couldn't," I pressed on, "then it's some place difficult to get at. Where abouts? Around here? Up north?" And as she kept her silence, "Oh, come on, Mary! You've told me this much—"

I saw then that she was gathering up her things, taking flight already, and shaking her head again as if the movement would strengthen her resolve. I had pressed too hard, and the result was going to be a blank.

When she was ready to go, she said, almost angrily, "You mustn't make people break their promises."

"I'm sorry. . . . No more questions, then. But don't go."

"I have to, anyway."

Her mood had changed completely; the easy afternoon had given place to the calculated business of the evening. To smooth over the transition, I said:

"Well, it was fun talking. Perhaps I'll see you later." I smiled. "As Joe would say, simmer down now."

"That Joe!" she answered viciously. "He's a snake! And those other two just need shooting! They're the meanest pair—"

"That's the way they're built."

She was suddenly glaring at me. "They don't have to act that way! Mr. Shepherd—" I had a moment's difficulty in recognizing the old man under the formal label—"Mr. Shepherd says they can't help it. That's not true!"

"But—"

"It's not true!" From some pent-up spring a torrent of argument burst out. "People are always saying they can't help it! If they steal a million dollars, they say they couldn't help it! If they get pregnant, they say it wasn't their fault! Even if there's a war, it's just too bad, it can't be helped. Baloney! Things don't just happen. It's *people* that do things, and they *can* help it!"

Before such vehemence I might have backed away with a soft answer. But a small demon from the realm of discord prompted me to ask:

"What about you, then?"

"What about me?" she snapped. "*I'm* not dreaming up any excuses! I've made my own life, and I'm not blaming it on anyone else! Anything that's happened to me is my own fault."

"Then that must go for the old man, too."

"What do you mean?"

"You've got to admit that he's been making a fool of himself lately. And it's been going on for a long time, hasn't it? He doesn't *have* to go down to the bar and stick his neck out. That's his own fault."

She sighed, losing the edge of her anger and her taut determination. "Oh, sure. . . . It's his own fault, all

right. . . . He can help it, but he doesn't want to.
. . . He says he's fishing." The strange word slipped
by us and away. Mary sighed again, a deeper, more
considered message from a compassionate heart.
"Don't think I haven't warned him. . . . He goes
on like this, they'll *crucify* him."

They crucified him that same night, with ease and
with appetite. I should have been there, perhaps to
make it less cruel, perhaps to stop the execution alto-
gether; but in fact I backed away from it, at the first
show of teeth, like any mangy dog. Excuses need time
to formulate, and careful thought to make them con-
vincing. At the moment of truth—which is a real
thing, not a by-product of the bull—I had none that
were not ignoble.

I had left my room about nine o'clock and gone
downstairs in the general direction of the bar. I talked
to the desk clerk in the lobby, and bought some cigar-
ettes, and stepped outside for a brief look at the stars
and two economical breaths of ice-cold air. Then I
crossed the lobby again, making for the swing doors,
and stopped in my tracks at the sound of a voice.

It was the expected voice, the known voice, shrill

and keyed-up, shouting, "This time you have gone too far!" Before I even had time to echo, in thought, Ed's words, "Here we go again," there was a crash of broken glass, a moment of silence, and then the same voice on a gasping note of denunciation:

"It's a horrible thought—that two thousand years of civilization—can only produce a brute like you! Perhaps we should—wipe out what we have done—and try again!"

I knew then that I was not going through that door into the bar for all the sunbeams in heaven. Indeed, I had turned away from it even before the excuses started queuing up in my mind. All I wanted was a quiet evening. By the sound of it, there were far too many people there. I didn't really need a drink. I had a drink up in my room, anyway. And why should I waste time with the same dreary scene when actually I had all this work to do?

Every sort of reason.

To the prudent music of "I know not the man," I climbed the stairs again and went back to my burrow.

It was Mary who roused me out, a half-hour later. She burst in without knocking; her face was distraught, her hair wildly tousled. The dress, torn at the shoulder, signed the completed picture with a sordid scrawl of violence. I rose from my typewriter, knowing that I was not going to escape after all.

"What's the trouble?"

The words came tumbling out. "They took him away! You must do something! They beat him up and took him away!"

"Who took him away?"

"The police."

I was conscious of relief; the news seemed a noticeable improvement upon the past. Mary continued to stare at me, as if she expected me to jump on a snow-white horse and gallop to the rescue with no more delay than a caper or two before the cameras. She was not yet up-to-date with the official mood of disengagement.

"Well," I said, "let's work something out. Sit down and have a drink, for a start."

"We haven't got time!"

I didn't like the sound of that at all; brisk movement was no part of the plan—nor was any other kind of movement. I crossed to the night table and poured myself a drink, very slowly, very deliberately. I had my own decisive scene to play, the one that solved everything and sent the audience home with a warm feeling that, after the troublemakers had done their worst, business trends were still up.

I said in a soothing voice, "There can't be all that hurry, if he's in jail."

"But we must get him out. Or he'll die."

She had sat down on the bed and was hitching the edge of her dress together with trembling fingers; she had taken, from me, the cue for calmness, but it was not yet within her compass. I poured her a drink, and she accepted it and gulped greedily; it was the first time I had seen her do anything save sip at her glass, a sip which consumed time more than liquor. Now her hands were reaching for her hair; her fingers became combs as she tried to set it to rights. She was doing her best to lower the temperature.

I said, like any stage uncle, "That's better. . . . Now tell me what happened."

She gathered her wits towards a reasoned story.

"He got in a row again, and Callaghan beat him up."

"Callaghan?"

"The big one."

The Ox. . . . "But how did it start?"

"Oh, Callaghan began picking on him. You know." Her face was drawn and hopeless as she re-lived the sequence. "He was waiting for him, because of what happened last time, when you. . . . He climbed right in, as soon as Shepherd came up to the bar. There was an argument, and Callaghan started to slap him around."

"Didn't anyone try to stop him?"

"Not this time."

"So?"

"Then he fell down, and Joe called the police."

The pronouns were mixed, but they could not mask the story. A thug had had his way, an old man had been beaten to the ground. The fact that I had heard the prologue to it myself, and had backed away, was beginning to tell. From the look of her, Mary had played a much more valiant part. . . . As if chiming in with my thoughts, she stood up again, and smoothed her rumpled dress, and said:

"You *must* help him."

Her voice had lost its strident edge; the tone was simple pleading. I reacted to it brusquely.

"Help him? How help him? What could I do?"

"Bail him out. Get him home somehow." Her hands

were clasping and unclasping, as if uttering small, urgent prayers. "He looked so terrible. . . . He looked nearly dead when they carried him out."

"They'll take care of him all right."

"They won't! The police here are awful. I know!"

I turned away. "Well, anyway. . . . It's out of my hands. It's got nothing to do with me."

"It has everything to do with you!"

"Oh, for God's sake!" I tried a scornful laugh, not too successful. "How do you figure that out?"

"Because of what's happened. Because you must be interested or you wouldn't have asked all those questions. Because you helped him the last time, and now he needs help again. More than ever. If you weren't sorry for him, you wouldn't have helped him the last time. Why did you help him, if you weren't interested?"

Why indeed? And how could an old man brutalized be less appealing than an old man merely threatened? The leaven of pity, the most insidious blackmail in all the world, was working against me. In face of it, a man could say, "No" only just so often. . . . But I stalled once more, in sulky defiance, the last refuge of the hard-driven male.

"It's his own fault."

"It's everybody's fault!" She came near to me. For some reason, undefined, the trap had sprung while I was looking elsewhere. It was as if she were handing me my coat and I were taking it without argument. She said again:

"You've *got* to help him."

5 JAIL DELIVERY

She had said that the Bone Lake police were awful.
They were. They were especially awful in the person
of the man in charge of the station that night, Sergeant
Labelle.

I am pro-police; my father was a policeman before
he became a soldier. But not all policemen brought
honor to the uniform. Canada had a wide range, from
the very top of the international credit tree—the
R.C.M.P.—down to a force not highly regarded in

our part of the world, where a corrupt political regime had steadily debased it over a space of twenty years to the level of a private strong-arm squad. Though the machine was now gone, the infection lingered. It was clear that it lingered most lovingly in the blood of Sergeant Labelle.

First impressions are best because they are the brightest; what comes after is likely to be staled by familiarity. This was a man I could never like; an oaf in authority, a man whom the insolence of office had rendered repellent. Some of it centered in his appearance, which of course he could not help; but even a big, fat man, a beer-and-beefburger man with his belly straining against a snake's-head belt, did not have to lounge at his desk as if he were the lord of creation.

He did not have to wear a stained and crumpled uniform which must, from the moment he put it on, have achieved scarecrow status. He did not have to pick his teeth; he did not have to have his cap on the back of his head; he did not have to look Mary up and down as though she were a piece of tainted meat which might, in part, prove eatable. Above all, he did not have to sigh as if our intrusion were intolerable, and lean forward, and growl:

"What is it now?"

Mary had sat down on a bare bench at one side of the cluttered, whitewashed room; Labelle's pig eyes followed her briefly before coming back to me. I met them with all the coldness which instinct prompted, and said:

"I've come about the old man."

At my direct words his glance flickered down and away, and he countered, too quickly, "What old man?"

"Mr. Shepherd."

"*Mister* Shepherd." The accent was an insult, and the pretense of consulting the papers on his desk was grisly. I waited while the sergeant went through this part of his act. Finally he sat back, lounging again, and said:

"Shepherd. . . . Well, well. . . . You a relative?"

"No."

"What's your name?"

"Peter Benton."

"Who d'you work for?"

"The Toronto *Journal*."

"Is that so?" There was a slight, a very slight

change of manner here: my paper was well-known; it had connotations of power and, above all, money. Labelle drummed on the arm of his chair for a few moments, thinking it out. Then ill nature rose above prudence. He said sarcastically, "Going to write us up?"

"No."

"Going to write about the old man?"

"No."

"Glad to hear it. Because you'd be wasting your time." He waited, but I said nothing. "Because Shepherd's just a jerk," he went on, much more roughly. "A troublemaker. A real sorehead." He was watching my face, hoping to come up with a word which would hit. When I still did not answer, he said, "Fact is, we've had just about enough of your friend."

I was going to answer, "He is not my friend," and then I thought—or I felt—that I should not use these words; not to smooth the situation, not to curry favor, not in any circumstances. In the pursuit of a quiet life I had gone far enough along that road already. Now the old man was hurt, and if there was one place in the world where he needed friends, it was here in this police station.

To deny him now would be like driving away from a road accident seen through the rear-view mirror. The pile-up is not one's own concern; it will waste time, it will ruin a schedule, it will mean questions and answers and probably blood on one's clothes. And yet one *must* stop, and turn, and bear a hand. Strangers bleeding to death can never quite be strangers.

I took my stand within this ring. "In the present case, my friend is not to blame."

"That's not the way I heard it." Faced with opposition, Labelle's eyes narrowed, and his fat jaw thrust forward into prominence. "He picked a fight, and he got hurt. It's not the first time."

I shook my head. "He was arguing, and the man he was arguing with lost his temper and beat him up."

"Then he shouldn't argue." Labelle leaned forward again. "Look, I don't have to waste time with this. Shepherd makes trouble. He's always doing it. This isn't the only complaint. If he goes on doing it, he'll end up in the morgue. I don't want him in my territory."

Territory, I thought—now *there* was a word. . . . I was watching Labelle; he was crudely conscious of his authority, and he didn't like me and he didn't like interference. Yet there was something in his manner which was less than ruthless; he couldn't help being tough, but he was holding back the full charge—as though he would not stand in my way if I fell in with his plans. There was a flaw somewhere, a discord within the harmony of arrogance. But before I could probe it, Labelle himself came some of the way to help me.

"Well, if you want him, that's *your* choice." He jerked his head backwards, towards a door behind him. "He's in there. You better take a look at him." And as I glanced from him to the door, surprised, he said, with a return of his full brutality, "You think I was going to carry him to the cells?"

Mary had already jumped up; she reached the door before me. I followed her into the narrow slit of a room which lay beyond.

I don't know what I had expected to see, but it was pitiful. The old man was sitting on the floor, propped up against the bare wall. There was blood on his coat and on the palms of his hands; a brutal weal down one side of his face had puffed out, thickening his lips, distorting the whole outline of his head into shapeless ugliness. His eyes were closed, and from the bruised mouth a whimpering sound came, a surrender to pain much weaker than a cry and far short of words.

Mary said, "Oh God!" and dropped on her knees, cradling his head against her breast. He gasped and almost screamed at the movement; the raw side of his face must have been in agony. Over her shoulder she called, "We've got to get him out of here. He'll die!"

I stood irresolute. I too wanted to take him in my arms and raise up that shattered form. But we had nothing to work with, not so much as a cup of water to bathe his wounds. I turned and went back into the larger room.

It was empty; where Labelle had been sitting, only a curl of acrid cigar smoke recalled his presence. For a moment I wondered if he were part of some evil dream, if there were, in truth and happily, no such man. While I was still wondering, he came back in again, by another door.

He had been washing his hands; now he was wiping them on a gray-white towel. He had a sullen look on his face, which told me that he was not going to speak until I did.

I said, "He can't stay here."

"You're damn right he can't!"

"You should have called a doctor."

"I got better things to do with my time." But something in my face must have shown the strength of my loathing and the path it might take. My hatred was nothing: but behind me he saw a rich newspaper, headlines, phone calls, paper work. I had met it before in people who, like pale slugs, needed the dark. He dropped the towel on the desk, and massaged his dry hands together, and said, "Look, don't make such a production. . . . He's O.K. . . . Good night's sleep, that's all. . . . You want him, you take him home."

I knew then that he wished for nothing more than to get rid of the whole thing, that he was afraid Shepherd would die on his hands. As long as the old man was only walking wounded, he could walk his way to the graveyard. . . . It would have been a fierce joy to refuse, to saddle Labelle with a dead body and a crushing guilt. But I could not do that, either.

"You're releasing him?" I asked.

"Yeah. Just keep him quiet, that's all."

"On bail?"

"No. We'll clean the whole thing up now."

It was a curious phrase and, within its framework, disgusting. A thousand men with a thousand mops could not cleanse this stable. But before I had time to guess what was in his mind, Labelle sat down at his desk and took up a pen. He drew a diary or logbook towards him, and with stubby fingers scored through some entry in it. Then he looked up at me again, as if he had done something clever and complicated, and said, "So far, so good."

"What about charges?"

He was curt. "There's no charges."

"What about charges against Callaghan?"

He had an answer for that, too. With invincible certainty he said, "Callaghan was provoked. We got witnesses."

It was hard to swallow, but somehow I managed it. "You mean, the old man can go free?"

"Just that."

I called to Mary, within the other room, "We're ready to leave," and there was a murmur, a stirring, another gasp of pain. I heard her say:

"Gently. Easy. . . . Let me help you."

I took a step towards the room, knowing I must be needed. From behind me came Labelle's voice:

"Hold on a minute. There's the court costs."

"Court costs?"

"Just that. He's been booked. Drunk and disorderly. Assault. Resisting arrest. I'm letting him go with a caution. But it's a legal process."

"How much?"

He scratched his jaw, eying me, weighing me up. "Three charges. Let's say—thirty dollars."

All I could think of was: Bone Lake must be growing up. The cops were crooked already.

"Can I have a receipt?"

"No."

"Why not?"

"You're a great one with the questions. . . . Because we don't give receipts, period. You want to pay the costs of the court? It's thirty dollars, cash money."

"And no receipt?"

"Just that." It had emerged as his favorite phrase. I wondered how much it had covered in the past, how many arguments it had clinched, how much dirt it had swept under the rug. I would have argued—my mouth was already opened for protest—but at that moment Mary came out of the back room, supporting the old man.

He looked dreadful—his knees buckling, his face a shambles, his skin the color of dirty water. There could be no argument on so pitiful a topic; any delay, any single word might snuff out the last of this candle. I put thirty dollars on the desk, and moved forward, and took a firm grip of the old man, hunching my shoulder under his. He felt like a bundle of sticks, and he smelled of fear and blood and old, old age.

Thus linked—could it be for the rest of his life? —we made for the doorway, a step at a time. When we reached the threshold, Labelle called out:

"Hey, you!"

I said, "Yes?" without turning my head.

"I wouldn't write it if I was you." His voice was loud, with a harsh confidence. "Don't forget—when you pull out, your friend will still be here."

He seemed even more my friend as we struggled through the doorway and out into clean air.

It was nearly midnight, and the clean air was also bitterly cold. Mary set our direction, which was across town, by streets carpeted with frozen slush and lined with shuttered stores, some derelict, all shabby. The full moon was our lamp; it shone with hopeful brilliance on broken windows, the poised daggers of icicles, the broken edge of a sidewalk, the snow trodden into dirty frosting or ploughed up into a bright furrow. It shone also upon us, the most dubious decoration of all.

I had feared that the old man would never make it; indeed, when we left the police station, it seemed likely that he would not manage more than a few steps before he came to the end of all his journeys. It would be a better death for him, under the glistening Pole Star, than on the bare floor of a police cupboard; but it would be death, none the less. Yet, astonishingly, the outside air did for him what it did for all of us; it touched his heart with hope and therefore with life.

His first few steps had scarcely been steps at all; even with help on either side, he had achieved no more than a baby's staggering gait. But he had improved with each wavering stride, as if he were learning to walk again and had shown himself a prodigy; starting as a child, he grew a whole year within the first fifty yards. Soon he was making fair progress; Mary dropped to one side, allowing him more freedom; and I had only to give him an occasional supporting arm to maintain a slow, steady headway.

He was also learning to talk again, which was not so welcome.

It was his old familiar tirade, made more nonsensical still by the alcohol, which the brisk air had not dispersed. He was wandering and muttering, making angry cries against unseen enemies, making pleas for understanding, making statements of great assurance on matters which had already slipped from his memory. Sometimes he sang, the old, sad songs which soldiers once found merry; sometimes he stopped dead, his legs astride the snowy pathway, and refused to go on until he had solved some interior riddle. He was an old man with too much on his mind, or not enough, and very soon I was sick of him.

When, for the fifth time, he came to a meandering stop and said, "I *know!* I *know* the secret! And now I'm dying!" I discovered that, in reaction, I was already bad-tempered. He was not unique; not even original. We were all dying, from the day we were born. I would learn nothing in this idiot company. . . . Mary came closer to him, trying to calm and comfort his despair; and presently he got going again, and I swallowed my irritation, and ranged up alongside, and gave him, once again, a helping hand. Living or dying, laughing or crying, we were all brothers still.

Yet I could not help lecturing. "You'd do better if you stopped talking and tried to concentrate."

At that moment he was walking normally, and now he nodded normally as if we were two wise men in agreement. He answered, with all the courtesy in the world:

"You may well be right. . . . In any case I am grateful for your assistance."

"Do it for me sometime."

But I had started a sudden new train of thought. "That's what makes the world go round!" he declaimed, flinging wide an arm which caught me on my half-frozen cheek and stung intolerably. "I do beg your pardon," he said loudly, and then began to sing. "The Golden Rule, you young fool," he sang, over and over again, to a measured air which presently I recognized as the chime made by a clock when it strikes the hour. His voice grew louder still, as piercing as a tuneless piano; the refrain changed to, "The Golden Rule, you damned fool!" A man—the sole passer-by in all our journey—stopped on the other side of the street and stared at us, a tall, grim guardian of propriety. It suddenly seemed an enormous waste of time to have lifted the old man out of one trouble, only to have him go staggering off into another.

I took a hard grip on his arm and said, "For Heaven's sake, keep quiet! Do you want to get arrested again?"

The thought, and my spiteful hold, penetrated. "By no means, by no means," he answered, in a voice which had now fallen to a whisper. He wiped his mouth, as if sponging away his offense. "You won't leave me, will you?"

I said, "I won't leave you, if you behave yourself."

He had not heard me. He pleaded again, "You won't leave me, will you? You cannot leave me!"

"All right. I won't leave you."

"A solemn promise?"

"A solemn promise."

"I believe you, as a man of honor." He nodded again, owlishly wise, and then said, like a child delaying its bedtime, "*Why* won't you leave me?"

"Because it would be wrong."

It was the simplest answer I could think of; it was, for me, a true answer, and I hoped it would calm him down. It calmed him down, indeed, to such an extent that he put his arm around my shoulder, like a kindly tutor, and said solemnly:

"I see that you share my moral sense. . . . Whenever you propose to do *anything*, you should stop and ask yourself, 'If everyone did this, what would the world be like?' You will soon discover the right answer."

Then, as if all strength had drained away with this advice, he fell at my feet in a dead faint. A dribble of blood darkened the snow as his head rolled loosely over. Cursing all folly—his and my own—I picked him up and set out to carry him the rest of the way. He was hollow-light, like an armful of kindling; but, on the slippery path under a moon which had now clouded over, it was a wearisome job. At a crossroads where I paused to shift his weight and my heavy snow boots crunched through a rime of ice, a dog barked. Our wretched caravan moved on.

It was with relief that I saw Mary, who was walking ahead, stop at last before a squat house on a dim street corner, and call out:

"We're home."

*

6
HOME, BE IT NEVER SO

Home, for the old man, was a two-down, two-up
rooming house which, though it must have been built
(like all of Bone Lake) within the last three years, was
already shoddy and run to seed. There were lights on
when we arrived—or, rather, there was one light,
deep within the echoing hallway; the moon outside
was far brighter and cleaner than this murky sentinel

which waited for us. The moon had shone down on a crazy sort of building, thrown together with cement blocks, tar-paper, and corrugated iron; the hallway, which was angular and dim, smelled of cooking—if burned fat is part of cooking—and a sour poverty.

The house was not even doomed to become a slum; it had started life as one. It looked mean, it smelled mean; and the only person stirring was the meanest thing about it.

She was a woman, grim and sallow and small, dressed (far out of her age group) in the kind of sloppy flowered housecoat worn by brides who have given up. She had sighted us first through what I guessed to be an ever-open crack in her door, and had come out very quickly to meet us in the hall. She stood staring at us, hands on hips, like a statue of watchful malice, as we came in—and, to be absolutely fair, we were not the kind of procession for which doormen bowed and managers trotted forward with a bunch of long-stemmed roses.

Mary wore a rumpled camel's-hair coat, wet with snow, bloodstained on one shoulder; I was dressed like the northland version of a newspaperman who is saving his money for better things; and I was carrying an old man, exhausted to the point of death, whose face under the lamplight was swollen, bruised, and caked with dried blood.

But still, I thought, she need not have faced us with such vile contempt. She need not have looked at the derelict old man and said with waspish, sneering satisfaction:

"I guess he's corned again."

For the first time that evening I sighed; a genuine, deep-felt sigh of exasperation. This was not my day. Around every new corner I blundered onto a battle-field; whatever I did, someone had been there first and booby-trapped the area. First I had run away from the old man, and he had caught up with me. Then I had set out to rescue him and collided with the police—and lost thirty dollars. Now I had carried him home, like any good Samaritan, and it seemed that I had done the wrong thing again and must explain my ignoble actions to this resident harpy.

I felt that even if I did something invincibly good, like pulling an orphan child from a hole in the ice, I would find myself behind bars, charged with loitering, trespass, damage to municipal property. . . . But patience was still a virtue, and the old man in my arms

was still real and pitiful. I summoned what spirit I
could and answered:

"He's had an accident. He's been hurt."

"So what's new?" The woman's rasping voice, like
her appearance, was the most unpleasant thing in this
unpleasant house. "He's always having accidents. . . .
Well, you can just dump him and get out of here."

Mary came forward. "He really is hurt," she said.
"He needs help."

The woman looked at her. "So it's you again," she
said with manifest spite. "Didn't I tell you to stay
away from here?"

"He needs help," said Mary again, more stub-
bornly.

"He needs his head examined. With an ice pick."

The old man chose this moment to come to his
senses. He did so swiftly; at one second he was the
stillest of still life, at the next he had stirred, and
slipped from my arms, and shaken himself like a
waking dog as he finally stood upright. He remained
a fearsome sight; the dim light did nothing for the
weal on his face save to make it more livid still, and
he wavered about on his legs in a slow, erratic circle,
the best he could manage in self-control.

"Mrs. Cross," he stuttered, and produced, to my astonishment, a sketchy bow. "Apologize for my appearance. . . . Met with a mishap. . . . My friends were kind enough. . . ." He waved his hand around in our direction; it was an introduction of sorts, though I had no inclination to bow myself. "Hope I haven't kept you up."

"That'll be the day." She was surveying the old man with relentless hatred; a disgusting slattern herself, she was made bold by her belief that she had found a worse human being. One could tell that she had grown sick to death of him, and yet she needed him also; she had to have him nearby, as a yardstick of misery and human decline. "You've tied one on again," she declared loudly. "Time you finished up in jail where you belong!"

Mary had moved forward again, protective in a way I had not yet matched, and taken the old man's arm. "Come on," she said encouragingly. "We'll get you upstairs."

Mrs. Cross glared at her. "Cheap trash!" she said. And then, "Where are you going, miss?"

"I'm taking him upstairs."

"I'll be waiting to see you come down!"

On the point of flight, I changed my mind. If Mary could prove herself brave against these degrading odds, so could I. I took the old man's other arm, and the three of us moved towards the bare cement staircase.

Mrs. Cross called after me, "Hold it! Where do you think you're going?"

"Upstairs."

"No visitors after ten o'clock. What do you think I'm running here?"

I was tempted to answer, and then thought better of it. She could outbawl me any time. . . . "He needs help," I said mildly, and kept on retreating.

As we made our escape, she shouted after us, "I'll be waiting for you! And keep the door open!"

Laboriously up the stairs we went, myself now supporting the old man, and Mary trailing behind us. The ascent was painfully slow; twice he had to pause for rest, once he fell and lay still in gasping despair. For some unholy reason I recalled another agonizing journey; the phrase "The Stations of Mrs. Cross" slipped into my mind unawares, before I could stop it. I had been brought up to hate blasphemy, and I still did so; the appalling lapse made me angry—or made me more angry still, because there had already been quite enough in that evening to turn all the milk of humanity sour. Even Mary, who must have been exposed to Mrs. Cross before, was muttering to herself, as if the new outrage had been more than she could bear.

But as we passed the threshold of his room, the old man put us both to shame. He looked closely into our faces, divining our disgust, and said:

"If we knew *all* about her, we would forgive her."

At any other moment, perhaps from any other man, it would have sounded false, like those phony answers to interviewers: "To what do you attribute your success in running this motel"—"Well, I guess I just love people." (Love people! One might as well say, "I just love liquid," as if it didn't matter whether one drank champagne or kerosene.) But the old man managed to give his words a positively saintlike conviction; it was clear that he really did mean what he said about Mrs. Cross, and that he himself had already forgiven her all things.

In the circumstances it was the most generous remark I had ever heard; and as soon as he had said it—as though its virtue had cost him dear—he staggered forward and collapsed upon his bed.

For the moment he was as well off there as anywhere else, and I did not move to help him. But he could not be left indefinitely.

"We ought to get a doctor," I said. "Is there one?"

Mary had come to the foot of the bed and was looking down at the old man with a world of compassion. "There is," she answered, "but he's off north somewhere. Mercy mission, but he got snowed in. They were talking about it at the hotel."

Well, I thought, we'll just have to run our own mercy mission. . . . I took a moment to look around the room. It was icily cold, and hardly furnished at all; a bed, a sagging armchair, and an unpainted pinewood chest was the total catalogue. Behind the door was a rucksack, hanging from its chafed and twisted straps; in one corner stood a pair of high-laced boots, the leather cracked, the toes curling upwards; on top of the chest was a metal coffeepot and a pair of silverbacked brushes, battered and scratched; the worn bristles were as yellow as corn. The iron bedstead was covered with what looked like an ancient army-surplus blanket; across one corner of its faded khaki was stenciled the word, "BLIGHTY."

Giving pitiful clues to the threadbare past, the room promised a most meager end to a long life.

I returned to the wretched proprietor of this castle. The old man, stretched out on his back, was stirring again. He was also moaning as his hand went to the ravaged cheek, which must, even in this chilly room, be thawing into agony. The rest of his body was shaking with cold.

"We've got to get him to bed," I said. "And get him warm somehow. This room's like a morgue."

"I'll make some coffee," said Mary obediently. "There's a ring at the end of the hall. But—" she looked around—"they must have taken away his heater."

"Then they'll bring it back." I was bending over the old man, gently wrestling him out of his clothes; he helped me as much as he could, baring his shivering body, which was wasted away to nothing, like a skeleton drawn with a single smudgy chalk line. It took a long time. Presently he whispered, "Nightshirt —pillow," and under the pillow I found a red-flannel shirt with a flapping tail—a veritable relic of the stately past. Finally I tucked him in under the blanket, still trembling violently, as Mary came back with a coffeepot which made a thin plume of steam in the bitter air.

I said, "Back in a minute," and went downstairs again.

I had expected a battle over the heater and was savagely ready for it; when I reached the entrance hall, the battle took place. There was no heater, said Mrs. Cross, looking at me with a malevolent stare as if I had demanded a mink stole on a silver tray. Well, there was a heater, but it didn't work—the old man had broken it. Well, there was another heater, but heaters cost money to run. Well, there was this heater, but it was five dollars a month, cash in advance. Well, there was *this* heater—and I hope you fall onto it and fry, her furious eyes said as she handed it over and I started up the stairs again.

She shouted after me, "And don't stay all night! Single room means what it says!" I had an idea that she would take the heater away again as soon as I was gone. But that would be another day, another field of battle.

For the moment, at an investment of thirty-five dollars, old Shepherd was home, and dry.

A sort of peace had come to the old man's room when I returned. He had drunk some of his coffee, and Mary had bathed his face; now she was rubbing his feet under the blanket while he lay back, his eyes closed. The room slowly warmed as the electric heater did its work. It was domestic tranquillity, of a sort; a moment when one could slip away without too bad a conscience. Thinking that he was falling asleep, I said softly, "If he's O.K., I'm on my way."

Mary nodded, not interrupting what she was doing, and I glanced around for my coat. When next I looked at the old man, he had sat up in bed, bright as a button, and was smiling at me. Then he said, without preamble:

"Were you in the last war?"

For a moment I thought he was babbling; then, meeting those sharp and shining eyes, I suspected this to be an odd social gambit—he wanted me to stay, for fear of loneliness, and thus had said the first thing that came into his mind. It was not till much later that I came to realize that this question of his, out of the blue, was the trigger for all that came after; that he had planned it that way, and with it, perhaps, the rest of my life. By such small beginnings—a smile, a shot, a single sentence such as "Follow me"—is a man's path determined; and sometimes we are lucky not to know it.

But all I did then was answer, "No. I was too young."

I said it defensively, as my generation often did, though without much reason. Old people seem to forget how long ago was their war. I was eight years old when it ended; brave as a lion, no doubt, but youngish for that contest. Yet I had something more reputable to add.

"But my father was killed in it."

His intent eyes rested on mine. "How?"

"He was taken prisoner in Hong Kong. Then he was killed on the Burma Road."

"We are wolves, wolves with the minds of men. . . . I was in both those wars, once as a boy, once as a man." (That made him about seventy, at least.) "I was a mole in the first, a trench mole. And then a weed, drifting to and fro across the Atlantic, in the second. But never a man with a brain."

He was looking at the ceiling now, his hands at the back of his head, regretting the past without rancor. I decided to give this only a few more moments. In the line of newspaper duty, I had heard old soldiers reminiscing before; they never needed an audience, even of one.

"Wasted years," he murmured. "Wasted people. . . . War is the most absurd game ever invented by the human mind and sustained by human appetite. But I should not lecture *you*. Young men don't make wars. They only fight them. Old men make wars— and survive them. They are immensely brave with other people's sons. But this time, there will be no such pattern. They have not come to realize that, yet. But they had better!"

I said nothing. I had heard this kind of talk a hundred times before, from well-meaning people; I believed in what they were saying, but not in their capacity to do anything about it. They would rally for peace; they would donate words and money and dogged patience and sometimes personal pride; and then somebody quite different would press a button, and they promptly fell apart. There had been people like that by the million—so the books assured us—in

1914, in 1939. But at the first sound of the drum, the audience drifted away and within an hour had picked up the step for war.

But old Shepherd was going on—and I realized that I had been wrong to think that he was recalling the past "without rancor," for when his voice started again it was suddenly harsh and compelling.

"They had better realize it," he said, "because next time there aren't going to be any men with brains, alive or dead. Babies with two heads and no legs, maybe. Men with bones already made of glue. Girls with a third breast." It was strange how these few words, in a thin, bitter voice, could conjure up for me a whole inferno of unspeakable creatures. "But no people as we know them. War won't be a game any more. It will be global cooking—making a soup of humanity."

Of course I agreed—who didn't?—and his words, and particularly the last phrase, had found their mark, both in myself and also in Mary, who had stopped rubbing his feet and was staring at him almost horror-struck. But mostly I agreed because of my father: I did not need anyone else's nightmares. My strongest childhood memory had been of my mother learning of my father's death and—later and far worse—of the sort of death it had been. A surviving friend of his, with the best of intentions, had made a long journey to talk to her, had got maudlin drunk, and told her a detailed story.

"*They jest at scars, who never felt a wound*" was never true thereafter in our small household. My father had been pulped to death by a Japanese sergeant trying out a new bamboo swagger cane. He had died praying, and then screaming, and, at the end, only twitching.

On that day and ever afterwards, when I thought of war I thought of my father dying sweetly for his country in that forest clearing, broken and re-broken for as long as he moved, and then stamped into the ground like a bloody reed mat.

Sometimes, on a street corner, a smiling oriental face would jog my memory.

Because I felt thus strongly, I answered the old man offhand. "You don't have to sell it to *me!* I don't want to die, not in anyone's quarrel."

He reacted to my tone, frowning as Mary was frowning. "That's not enough! You must want to live!"

"Oh, I do, I do. . . . Look, it's getting late. I must go home."

Mary said suddenly, "Don't be such a smart aleck."

I didn't think I deserved that, but I wasn't going to tell either of them about my father. I got up without a word and began to put on my coat.

"Stay," said the old man anxiously, as if some plan were going wrong. "I have more to tell you. . . . About the end of the world. . . . It has happened once already, I can prove it. . . ." He seemed to be wandering again, losing his grip; I realized that his wits ebbed and flowed like any other tide. "I can show you a sign. . . . I will tell you my secret!" I thought he was growing wilder still, but suddenly he calmed down, and his eyes grew lucid. "I will really tell you. And you are the last person I shall tell."

I shook my head. "I don't need to be told." Though he sounded sane enough, I thought he might be confusing a lot of different things, that this would turn out to be some sort of Mad Trapper story, the Hidden Treasure of Baffin Island in six instalments. There were scores of them current in the northland; they mostly featured a lost mine and a man who came into town with a sackful of gold, then went back for more, never to be seen by mortal eye again. "You don't have to tell me anything," I said again. "Why not settle down and get some sleep?"

But Mary was frowning at me again, and the old man was pushing on, brushing aside all objections. "You need to know *this!* Not one person in the world has believed me so far, except—" he nodded to Mary —"perhaps you. But I shall try once again." He was looking at me steadily. "You are young, as well— young and good-hearted. Perhaps you will believe it, and perhaps you will do something about it." Half-in and half-out of my coat, I tried to interrupt again; but before I could get a word out, the old man asked quickly, "Do you know what the Dew Line is?"

I was ready to be irritable. "Of course I do."

"But do you know what it stands for?"

"Distant Early Warning."

"Quite so. . . . I can show you another sort of Dew Line. A very distant early warning. The earliest of all."

This didn't make any sense, but in spite of my resolve I asked:

"You mean, you think there was a Dew Line before?"

"I would not doubt it." For some reason his voice held a tinge of sarcasm. "But this is something different. A discovery. . . ." His voice was becoming charged with excitement, and his head lifted from the pillow. "I discovered something which proved that everything has happened before, that this is not our first time on earth. . . ." He saw my face, disbelieving, not ready to listen much longer, and he grew desperate. "I tell you, I can prove it! I can prove it because of something I found up on Bylot Island, at the very top of Baffin. One of the most desolate places in the world! Scarcely habitable even now! Scarcely visited! But it has been used before!"

"Used?"

"Used by skilled men, men of science!"

"What did you find, then?"

He nursed his secret for a moment more; long years, much mockery had made him a jealous guardian. Then he said, calmly and quietly:

"I found a colossal refrigerator. And it was full."

7

THE GREAT ICEBOX

Who could have left at such a moment? Not I. His bizarre words touched a number of chords; some of them had to do with my job, but getting a good story was not what made me stay and listen. It was already something deeper and more important to me; something grounded in my own past, some need unfulfilled, some quest not yet undertaken. I felt, as strongly as I had ever felt before, that if I went away without hearing what he had to say—however strange, however nonsensical—I would never log my due ration of experience, I would never really catch up.

I had felt the same sort of thing on a more light-hearted plane in the past; the conviction that if I left a party early, I would lose something worth while; that if I didn't kiss a certain person, I would be short of one girl for the rest of my life; even that if I missed a television show, I would miss it forever.

Such things can scarcely ever be true; but I had the same feeling now, and this time it was not related to a significant meeting, a pretty girl, a classic performance. For some reason I knew that a stage had been set for drama on a grand scale. I had been invited; if I walked out, I would be a traitor to my own future and would mourn the fact forever.

It was very late, on an Arctic night far from home; an apt moment for wayward fancy, a moment not to be trusted, not to be measured against the cold reason of broad daylight. But I did not hesitate. To do so would have been like edging away down a side alley of history, turning one's back on the Battle of Waterloo, the murder of Caesar, the Birth at Bethlehem. . . . A web of such fantasies seemed to be brushing the inside of my skull. Common sense was overdue. I hung up my coat behind the door, on top of the shabby rucksack, and sat down in the armchair.

"What do you mean?" I asked. "You must explain."

"It's a very long story."

He was still sitting up in bed; he was not less eager than when he had made his last plea for me to listen, but his pale, exhausted face showed what an effort it had been to capture my attention. Some doubt of his strength must have shown in my face, for he smiled gently and said, "If Mary brings us some more coffee, I promise to last out the night."

She was off in a moment, and back very soon, with the re-heated coffee; silence ruled the room and indeed the whole house, for when Mary returned and shut the door behind her, she said, "I guess she's gone to bed." There was only one enemy *she* in our lives. . . . The old man settled back again; Mary sat at the foot of the bed; I made myself as comfortable as I could in the wrecked armchair.

I was watching old Shepherd with close attention.

He had changed notably; in particular he was no longer the man I had first seen in the hotel bar, using words like *idiot* and *animal*, losing his temper, flogging a sodden brain and still failing to find the right phrase. Of course, over the last few hours the liquor had ebbed away, but this was more than a sobering up. In some way he had been purified.

Pain seemed to have brought him to his senses, and his senses were delicate and subtle. A drunken, babbling man no longer lived in that frail body; he had been exorcized, and in his place was another man, old and wise, who had an important story to tell and who could tell it skillfully, in exactly the way it should be told. Whether it was an effort for him, I did not know, any more than I knew how long he had to live. But if *he* knew how long, the knowledge might be the spur, the agent of precision.

His voice was thin and reedy, and sometimes it paused and sometimes it faltered. But one forgot the man very soon. Like the best of the boxing referees, one hardly realized he was there at all. He did not come between us and the facts; the facts stood revealed under a naked light, on the very apron of a fantastic stage.

Nearly a quarter of a century earlier [*said the old man*] he had come to this part of the world for the first time. He had been, of all things, a ship's doctor for a company which ran small freighters from Liverpool and Bristol to the eastern seaboard of Canada and the United States. It was not a good company. Its ships were old, patched up, disgracefully staggering to and fro on their last sea legs. Always there came a day when they finally refused duty, and whenever that happened, they were sold as scrap or left to rot.

Shepherd's last ship chose the port of Churchill, on the western side of Hudson Bay, for her everlasting graveyard. She had suffered a prolonged engine breakdown; winter caught her and she was iced in; the ancient hull failed under pressure and began to fall to pieces at the quayside. There were claims and counterclaims, a bankruptcy, an insurance wrangle, a repudiation of liability; far from home, the crew was orphaned and abandoned. Most of them, cared for with that special public generosity which sailors can count on all the way around the globe, found their way back to England. Shepherd stayed where he was.

He had been a doctor by accident; it was the most recent of many careers; he was fifty years of age; he could still, he felt, be anything or nothing. In the spring he began to wander north and northwest, turning his hand to any odd job that came along—construction, prospecting, trapping, fishing, guiding; living with the Eskimos or by himself, learning his way about. He was looking for something. As long as he did not know what it was, he need not acknowledge failure, and thus was happy.

"Part of it was probably the so-called 'lost mine,' " he admitted, almost shamefacedly. "Or the hidden valley, like Shangri-La, when you climb a mountain, and descend a glacier, and find yourself suddenly in a secret garden of trees, grassland, flowers, temperatures of seventy and eighty degrees. . . . There are many such legends. They persist, and they do no harm."

He did not find his fabulous lost mine; he never stumbled into Eden. Colder climates, harsher journeys beckoned him again; the pride of manhood had then been very strong. He crossed the Hudson Strait into Baffin Island, and the shores of Foxe Basin. He pushed further northwards, sometimes with other wanderers, sometimes alone; by now he was an expert at staying alive in this hardest of countries. He passed the far-off spine of mountains which were the crown of Baffin.

He reached the northern tip of the island. He joined some Eskimos in a whaleboat, crossing to Bylot Island. Then there was a quarrel, and he was alone again.

Bylot was then an empty land, most desolate, topped by the noble peak of Mount Thule, more than six thousand feet nearer Heaven. Somehow he wintered there, the worst winter of his life. When spring came and he felt strong again, he began to look about him.

Throughout that long winter he had constantly been attracted by a faraway mountain of ice, not part of Mount Thule, but towering by itself on the northern coast. It was one of several, like a line of distant white battlements. Their shapes were serenely perfect, as if they had been hand-sculptured—though the hand was Time itself, and the span of the hand might have been a million years. Shepherd set out to take a closer look; he lost his way in a three-day snow blizzard, and when the weather cleared, he was high above sea level and had reached the base of one of the ice castles—he was not sure which.

One wall of it seemed to have been eroded; there were climatic changes hereabouts which, over an enormous number of years, were doing unpredictable things in the Arctic. In this case, a slope of the icecap had melted, leaving bare a natural pathway leading to a breach in the icewall. Shepherd took the curved pathway, because it was easier and he needed rest and shelter.

When he turned the last corner, he met a man.

"Oh, a dead man," said Shepherd, answering my astonished look. "He was standing on guard before the breach in the icewall; leaning back against one side of it, frozen there forever."

"Was he an Eskimo?" I asked. It was the first time I had interrupted.

"No. Not an Eskimo. Very different, facially. He was small and dark. And naked."

"Naked? In that cold?"

"This man did not need clothes. . . . Have you ever seen an armadillo?"

"Yes."

Well, the small man had been like an armadillo; his skin was scaly, but perfectly armored and jointed. He seemed to have been frozen, not by death but by horror or amazement; his eyes were narrowed, and his hand was up to protect them—as if he had seen some hideous burst of light on the far horizon.

Shepherd had the clear impression that he had walked out of the breach in the wall, and straight into a shock wave which, balked by a mountain, could strike a man dead.

Or it might have been, he thought, some kind of selective weapon which took care of human beings and also took care—in another sense—of their property. At any rate, the scaly man was dead, and the ice castle he guarded was intact.

Shepherd, whose nerves had been toughened by solitude, edged past the dead man and moved inside. He found himself in a small rock chamber which must have served as a kind of guardroom, for there were the scaly man's companions—six of them, seated on a bench at a long table, frozen in the same bizarre way. They sat in graded attitudes of wakefulness, ranging from the man nearest the door, whose fists were on the table as if he had been rising in alarm, to the man furthest away, his head still sleepily sunk in his hands. Even the faces they showed were carefully graduated; the nearest man was full-face, the last man in profile. It must all have happened in a few seconds of time. The man standing at the doorway, perhaps, had been the most alert of this unearthly crew.

It was not dark inside, though the guardroom was windowless; as Shepherd moved, something—probably his body heat—triggered an eerie glow from the floor, which was of some opaque material like roughened Fibreglas. The same thing happened when he walked past the dead guards and into the room beyond. But the room beyond was truly fantastic.

He found himself inside a vast hollow mountain of iced rock, an arched cathedral literally miles long. It was clear, immediately, what the place was; a huge refrigerator crammed with food. It was constructed on many floors; its bays stretched away into the darkness, though once again, as Shepherd walked forward, the floor lights came on in a thirty-foot circle all around him, and a corresponding light answered from the roof. The bays were so immense that he never reached the end even of one of them; he estimated them to be at least ten miles long. He guessed that the place was lit, and powered, by solar heat. There was a fleet of enormous trackless trolleys which began to move when he stepped on them; they moved in whichever direction he was facing. Whole storeys changed position, up or down, as soon as a hand was stretched out.

Of course, he did not discover this all at once; it took endless experiment before he had mastered the control system—or even part of it.

"I spent hours—days—practicing with the various mechanisms," he said. "It was like playing trains—with trains. It took me a long time to notice that the trolleys moved faster when I spread my feet apart. Then I discovered that whichever floor—well, they were huge shelves, really—whichever shelf I pointed at directly, with a straight arm, came down noiselessly to my own level for unloading onto the trolleys. Then when the trolley moved away, the whole system of shelving went back to its normal position. It was immensely ingenious. We certainly could not match it at our present stage."

He constantly stressed this—that the place reflected a technological standard far in advance of our own. And if other proof of an incredible antiquity were needed, it was in the food itself.

Some of it was modern, in the sense that it could be recognized; other categories could only be guessed at; the endless galleries of ancient yet sophisticated food, in this whole city of provisions, continued to astonish him wherever he explored. There were jars of oil and wine. There were towering silos of some kind of grain. There were millions of loaves of bread on racks. There were tubs of pressed meat. There were huge carcasses, birds and animals of unknown shape—he noticed one vaguely like a mammoth, but with a great flaring snout instead of a trunk, another like a hen, but a hen as big as an ostrich, with four wings and four legs. ("Like the bumblebee," said Shepherd with a faint smile, "it was aerodynamically impossible.") There were acres and acres of fish the size of fat cattle, very carefully graded in weight and perhaps in quality; he guessed that they were part of a controlled herd, probably grazed underwater on beds of kelp.

"I found that idea heartening," he said in parenthesis. "Because it was so promising for our own future. These people seemed to have tapped the riches of the sea and brought them under control, as we control the soil now. Those fish had been bred and raised in underwater pastures. . . . There were other things, concentrates, from the same area." He smiled again. "I thought I was very brave when I ate some."

A question was irresistible. "What did it taste like?"

"Seaweed. But a mouthful of it satisfied my hunger for a whole day."

Now, it seemed, he was nearing the end of his account; his voice was weakening, and his face gray with exhaustion. At one point he appeared to have fallen asleep, and we had to wait many minutes until, unprompted, he took up his story again.

He spent more than two months in the great icebox, exploring, mapping, taking notes, making sketches. He never discovered how these stores were listed or labeled; he saw no writing of any kind, but there were a large number of soft-metal plaques set into the floor, each bearing a certain number of indentations arranged in various shapes. It was possible that this was some kind of card-index system, which an expert could read at a glance. The only human bodies he discovered were those of the original seven men; he thought it probable that there were other entrances and other guardrooms which he did not reach.

The ice mountain was on the very edge of the coast, but there were no traces of any harbor installation. However, the water level had dropped more than a thousand feet, bearing over the centuries everything movable with it. Shepherd conjectured that outside distribution might have been by air, handled from launching platforms on the ice. He spent weeks of pondering on such riddles; considering the intricacies of the icebox, it did not seem that the men who could build an instrument of such complexity would have any difficulty in solving their logistical problems.

"I found it very sad to leave," he said towards the end. His voice had slowed and sunk to a murmur. "The place had an unbelievable fascination, even though to be alone in its vastness seemed to reduce me to the status of a pigmy—a jungle pigmy in a terrifying urban canyon. I wanted to grow, to master it, and to enjoy it forever. . . . But I had to remind myself that there were problems which twentieth-century man had not solved—such as getting home again in an Arctic winter. And of course I was wildly impatient to tell the world about it. . . . On the last day I made up a package, as much as I dared carry, of some of the smaller items. I had a last run on one of the trolleys, up to the outer doorway. Then it was time to go.

"As I left, I touched the shoulder of the small scaly man, for luck. How I longed to question him. . . . I needed luck, I can tell you, on that journey back."

He paused now for a long time. His eyes were closed. When he opened them, he was staring directly at me.

"You see what this means, don't you? It is a clear warning from the past. It means that there was a sophisticated world of applied science, millions of years ago, which all but vanished. There can be no other explanation. That world reached at least the same stage as we have now, and then it destroyed itself. Why? Because it discovered more than it knew how to use. So have we. It happened then, and it can happen now, unless we retreat from it. Like them, we have only one more step to take."

I was stupid with prolonged concentration and lack of sleep. "What happened then, exactly?"

He muttered, almost testily, "I told you—the last of their wars, and the end of their world."

Then he fell silent again. Presently his breathing grew deeper, and his head fell to one side, and he was at last at rest.

It was dawn when I stood up; the pale light, falling on the bed, showed the old man's hands paper-thin on top of the blanket, and his face sunken and deeply lined. He would talk no more that night. I stretched, and found that my whole body was aching; my head fluttered emptily and then, a moment afterwards, felt as if it would burst if it were burdened with a single thought more. I wanted to live some time, very quietly, with this story before I came to grips with it.

Mary said two things to me in farewell. One was: "I will stay and watch," and the other: "You must believe him, Peter." The last appeal, in a voice as small as conscience, followed me as I went stiffly down the stairs and out into the brilliant cold.

﹡

8 IF IN DOUBT

"He's very sick," wrote Mary in a scribbled note which reached me at the hotel. *"But wants to see you as soon as he can. Will let you know."*

So, for two days, I waited, and was secretly glad of it, and spent the time trying to come to terms with what I thought and felt and believed about the old man's story. I found that, somewhere between the personal and the professional planes, a split had already developed, and that the split was right down the middle of what I was entitled to call my soul. It was as fundamental as that.

Of course, as a newsman, I didn't believe a word of what he had said; to hear and then to reject such stories was one of the ways I earned my living. It was no reflection on him. . . . All sorts of people thought they had come across an earth-shaking story; at times it seemed that half the world wanted to catch you by the sleeve and tell you about the flying saucer in the back garden. It was often impossible to distinguish where the core of fact ended and the lunatic fringe began. Even in a short career, I had already encountered some beauties.

Moreover, these were only the self-deluders. There was, also, an army of liars who saw their names in print as part of the illuminated missal of history.

One developed over the years a certain hard-boiled cynicism; it was often a newsman's best armor. It did not make him a better person, but it allowed fewer mistakes in an area where mistakes showed up in plain black and white, adorned with a red face rampant. I had come *not* to believe in the lost jewelry of film stars, or the marriage of true minds between a rich woman of fifty-five and a youthful European noble-man. I had serious doubts about the little old lady who stole to buy milk for her retarded grandchildren; and a resolute disbelief that a thug who robbed and kicked to death his victim was acting out some childish trauma and should be asked not to do it again.

Great strokes of philanthropy never accidentally leaked to the newspapers. Evangelists did not sell out Madison Square Garden to the exclusive glory of the Lord. Love affairs never became notorious by chance; they were the domain of exhibitionists who often showed what they could do in public because they were no good anywhere else. There were scarcely any blind beggars, and no reluctant dictators at all.

One could enlarge the area indefinitely; one often had to; from love and politics it slopped over easily into commerce. There was no such character as an insurance man who bled his company white in order to safeguard your future. I could not believe that new cars were fabulous one year, rubbish the next. There were no sales of furs at sacrifice prices.

Above all, there were positively no old men who discovered million-year-old refrigerators beyond the Arctic Circle.

On the *Journal* we had an officially inspired motto: "*If in doubt, check.*" They were always hammering it in, particularly where the juniors were concerned; they even had it printed on cards, like the silly signs that said "THINK!" or (for funny people) "THIMK!" or (for funny U.S. presidents) "THE BUCK STOPS HERE." So I checked with the man who was always hammering it in the hardest; Bill Bradman of the *Journal*. It was high time for me to do so because, in spite of all the warning signals, I *was* in doubt, the greatest doubt of my life so far.

When I put through my call to Bradman, I found that he, at least, had not changed.

"How's the boy reporter?" was his greeting. He always said this; it always infuriated me. But that was not the reason he used these words; it was because he actually thought that I saw myself as some apprentice wonder-child of the newspaper world. That made it more infuriating still. Many such half-truths have this amount of penetration.

I returned his greeting, not too enthusiastically, and we talked for some time about the work in hand. Bradman did not sound in too much of a hurry, and he wasn't pressing me for delivery—which was one of the reasons why I liked working for the *Journal* and for him; if they trusted you with a story, they trusted you to produce it when it was ready. It was a no-nagging paper. But he did ask if I had any more trips to make and when I would be back.

"I don't know," I answered—and it sounded so inadequate, even to myself, that I had to improve on it. "I've got what I came for, I guess. But there's always a chance of another story."

"Another story, another time." He had grown a little more businesslike. "You know what I want the series to cover. Don't go steaming off into the blue looking for the abominable snowman. We've got him right here already—" and he mentioned a cabinet minister for whom he had less than total respect. "If you've got enough material, bring it back and let's take a look at it."

"There might be something else worth while." On the verge of talking about it, I suddenly wanted to skirt around the subject. "I met someone up here. . . . Have you ever heard of a man called Shepherd?"

"Yes," he said curtly.

"Well, I met—"

"What do you mean, a man called Shepherd?" he interrupted me, with a prompt show of bad temper. "Strewth, there must be a million of them! There must be twenty thousand Shepherds in Canada! What sort of question is that? Which Shepherd? Who? Where?"

"I just wondered if you'd heard of an old man called Shepherd. I met him up here."

"Give me strength!" he said, and sounded as if he meant it. "An old man? That narrows the field by about ten per cent. . . ." Then, when I did not answer, he seemed to check himself, and asked, "What's all this about? Are you on to something, boy?"

"I might be. He's an old man. He's lived up here a long time. He knows the North. I think he's Canadian, but he might be English. I wondered if you'd heard of him."

"Could be." I could almost hear Bradman scratching his ear with his pencil, which was his trick when thinking hard. "Shepherd? Shepherd?" He was dredging up Shepherds from a cloudy pool labeled *S*. "There was a hockey player called Shepherd. Henry Shepherd. No, he runs that girlie bar in Montreal.

There was Paul Shepherd and the woman in the car trunk. They hanged him. . . . There was Bishop Shepherd, out in Manitoba somewhere. Is this one a bishop?"

"No."

"Shepherd. . . . What does he do?"

"Nothing much, now. He used to explore, make trips up north."

"You're a big help. . . . There was a Shepherd involved in that timber-concession swindle in Vancouver. But he's sitting it out in Mexico. . . . Couldn't be Grant Shepherd. He's dead. Must be."

"Who's Grant Shepherd?"

"Don't you kids know anything?" demanded Bradman, with a return of ill temper and the habitual unfairness of the old. Give us time, I thought; one fine day we will grow into human shape. . . . Then his private filing system came into play, the capacity which I envied above all things. "Grant Shepherd went to jail for threatening the Russian delegate at the United Nations. Just after the war, when the Iron-Curtain thing started. About 1948. He tried to get their ambassador to read something, or look at something, and then he started raising Cain. He wouldn't promise to keep away from U.N. headquarters, so they locked him up till he cooled off. Don't you remember?"

"In 1948 I was eleven."

"Hell, it was on the radio. . . ." But under his irritation was a professional alertness. "You think you've met Grant Shepherd?"

"It sounds like it."

"He's probably a nut case by now. What's this all about, anyway?"

"Oh, he was telling some stories." For no reason at all I had now panicked; I could not bring myself to tell Bill Bradman what the old man had said. I would not expose him to another range of unbelievers. "I'll have a second session with him, and see if it works out."

"I wouldn't waste much time on him."

"O.K." But it was not quite possible to leave it thus. "Did you ever see him?"

"No."

"But did people believe him?"

"The police didn't. . . . What do you mean, believe? What is there to believe, anyway?"

"He wants to stop another war."

"Him and me both. . . ." There was a crackling sound on the long wire between Bone Lake and Toronto, and the volume began to fade. It seemed to mark the return of isolation for me, and I was wholeheartedly glad of it. Bradman said something which I could not make out, and then I heard his last words: "Whatever it is, it had better be good."

I was beginning to believe that it was. Indeed, from that very instant, the process of interior separation began. The phone call had taken care of one aspect, the hard-boiled professional side—what Mary had labelled "smart aleck." When I put the receiver back on its hook, faith flooded in, and took over.

It is time to say a little more about myself; not too much—just enough to make sense. It is the only way I can explain what now began to take hold, as the enormous and shattering effect of the old man's story broke through, and became impossible to subdue.

My short voyage started with the home, where all things must start; a home from which my father, deeply loved, desolately mourned by my mother, vanished at a single stroke. But she was not made bitter by this loss: although his hideous death, when she learned about it later, struck her to the heart, the heart was never vanquished. After the first paralyzing shock, she set herself (as I know now) to repair the damage; the damage to herself, to an only child whose face was a permanent question mark ("Who is God?"— "What's for supper?"), and to our small ship which had met this wicked storm. To have a brave widow for a mother can never be a handicap. In my case it furnished a bright faith to grow on.

Her rule was mostly negative, mostly *not*—and it was none the worse for that. If you can form the habit of *not* being a liar, *not* being a thief, *not* being cruel, and *not* kicking people in the face as you go up the ladder, you must be somewhere on the path to Heaven. It was Heaven my mother intended me to aim at; there was no mistake about that, either.

In our house religion was not "strict," any more than breathing was strict. It was necessary and natural; it was part of every day; it made irrefutable the fact that unless God cherished every heartbeat, a human being—and above all a boy—could only wander the world as an outcast, an envious starveling watching other people's birthday parties. God ruled the world and loved us all. I believed that, and I believe it still, in spite of awful evidence to the contrary. To try to reverse that evidence, in small ways and in large, was what we owed in return.

From all this, and especially from my father's death, it was natural that war was the most hated image in our lives. War denied Christ; it denied humanity; what in the world was left to justify it?

But although throughout my adult life war had been an urgent possibility, I had draped all my thinking in an obstinate flag of truce. War was wicked; no quarrel could be just; "the bomb" was the most wicked item of all; if good men forswore it, it would go away. Wrapped in this cosy moral blanket, I had settled for neutrality.

My mistake—as from today, astonishingly, it had become a mistake—was in thinking that one pious resolve was enough to clear the conscience. Of course it was not, and of course it solved nothing. Such resolution needed friends, converts, allies—by the score, the hundred, the thousand, the million. This, I now began to realize, in a slow-burning flash of recognition, was the lesson of the old man's story; unless we took to heart his sort of warning, we were all doomed. The story dovetailed so neatly with what

I felt and believed that its impact, if accepted, could only be fantastic.

Once I had absorbed it, I could not escape it. For a hundred reasons I knew that it would hang around my neck forever—or until I did something about it. What one man could do to reverse history, to cure such infection, was not yet imaginable. But I would have to think of something, or be branded a runaway forever.

One could run away from war, but never—not even with the rags of honor—from the prospect of peace.

On the second night, thus cornered by conscience, I took my troubles, like many a better man before me, down to the bar.

The jukebox was playing *Lonesome Road;* I wished I had laid a bet on it, particularly since it seemed that they were now playing it for me. I had had four drinks up in my room already and was in a take-your-choice mood; ready to be sad and sorry for myself, ready to argue about anything, ready for a laugh. It was the day before the midmonth pay day, and the

bar was nearly empty. The Ox—Callaghan—and the
Weasel propped up one end of it. Two men were
playing checkers at a side table, and two others
watching them. Joe was at his position of trust behind
the counter. Then there was me, and that was all. A
festive evening at Bone Lake was under way.

I got my drink and asked Joe about Ed the pilot,
whom I wanted to see.

"He's gone after the doctor, up at Frobisher," Joe
told me. "They've had plenty trouble up there."

"When will he be back?"

Joe shrugged. "Anybody's guess. The way I heard
it, they were snowed in again. But good." He looked
at me guardedly. "How's the old man?"

"Not too well."

"You want to get the doc for him?"

Down at the far end of the bar, the other two were
listening to us. The raw antennae which were now
part of my equipment, where the old man was concerned, began to come alive. I said:

"He could use a doctor. But it may be too late."

Joe gave the counter a swab and a polish, carefully
watching his own hand as it moved to and fro. Then
he asked, "How's that?"

"He's very sick. The way he was when he left here."

"That's too bad," said Joe.

Down the length of the bar, Callaghan raised his voice. "Labelle said he was walking O.K. when he left the station. Said he looked fine."

I didn't answer that one, but sipped my drink and stared at nothing. They were all guilty, and they knew it. I wasn't going to help them out. The silence settled around us, full of second thoughts.

Callaghan spoke again. "They say you're taking care of the old man."

The fifth strong drink was having its effect. For me, there could be no more denials. I saw now where I was going. If it could happen to St. Paul on the road to Damascus, it could happen to me at Bone Lake.

"Yes, I'm taking care of him. It's time somebody did."

The Weasel said, with a snigger, "You taking care of the girl, too?"

I didn't answer that, either; the joke fell, like the traditional lead balloon, flat on the floor of the bar. Callaghan half-turned towards his friend and growled,

"Knock it off, you!" and then came back to me. "What's the trouble with the old man?" he asked.

"You should know. You hit him."

But Callaghan had already been tampering with the evidence. "I didn't hit him. Not the way I could. I gave him the back of my hand, that's all. And he asked for it! I've got witnesses for that."

I said, "He's seventy years old."

"That's what's wrong with him, then. We've all got to go, sometime."

Joe came up with a fresh glass and a prompt salute. "Have this one on the house."

I took it, and justified it in the same moment of time. Let it be my farewell to the corrupt world. I leaned back against the bar and said:

"He's not dying of old age. He's dying of a crack on the side of the face, and lying about in the police station without a doctor, and walking a mile home when it was fifteen below zero. He's dying of brutality and neglect. He's dying for you." I had meant to say "because of you," not "for you," but that was the way it came out. I raised my glass and finished, idiotically, "So cheers!"

In the foolish silence after that, Callaghan said, "Sounds like old age to me."

At his side, the Weasel nudged him and then called out to me, "Your girl friend wants you."

Mary was standing in the doorway, looking towards me. I had not seen her for two days; I had forgotten how shabby and second-rate she looked, how poor an ally. But this was something else that I would not worry about, nor relate to the merit scale of the past. Mary need not pass any family inspection; my friends didn't have to be jealous. She was a fellow believer. I walked over to the door, and to her.

"How is he?"

"Not so good." She glanced towards the others, and then back to me. "He wants to see you, though."

"It's mutual."

The eyes in the thin face narrowed sharply. "If you're going to be cute—"

I said, "I'm going to listen to him. That's all I want to do, now."

Then I took her arm, and we walked out together. It did not even feel strange. No couple on their way to visit Shepherd could ever be ill-matched.

*

9
A LITTLE NIGHT MUSIC

The room was the same; the old man was not. He had changed shockingly in the brief time since I had last seen him; then he had been tired and freshly wounded, now he was riven by pain and exhaustion. When I came into his room, he was lying back against the gray pillows with his eyes closed; he was transparently pale, and the bony face had shrunk down to a pinched mask. The faded blanket on the bed seemed like his graveclothes, and the brave word "BLIGHTY" a label on a package ready for dispatch.

But the man himself was brave, as I knew by now; when he heard the door shut he opened his eyes, and even leaned forward to greet me. Then he began to talk, straightaway, without wasting time, as though he realized that time was not there to waste. He talked, also, as if he knew already that I believed.

Mary sat on the bed, holding his hand; I sat in the armchair, as I had done before; we were probably the most attentive audience he had ever had. I don't think that either of us had any choice. In that wretched room, on that wretched bier, he grew in authority even as he weakened. There were long pauses, but except for a couple of times when I wanted something explained or a detail added to a phrase I did not understand, I never thought to interrupt.

What he said, I have set down as I remember it.

He said, "I have thought for a long time about the people of that world. In fact I've thought about it for nearly a quarter of a century. We can deduce a great deal from the refrigerator and its contents. Here was a whole city of food, perhaps a hundred square miles. It was the sole survivor of world destruction—but

what a survivor! After millions of years, it was still in
working order; the solar power—or perhaps it was
atomic—still functioned perfectly; the vast stores
were intact; and it was all controlled by a handful of
men. For all we know, they may have been specially
bred for the job. But certainly there were very few of
them. The process of automation was complete.

"It shows how amazingly far they had advanced;
much farther than the meager inch of *our* earliest
history—the hot water and the central heating of the
Romans, the celestial accuracy of the Chinese or the
Druids. These people were infinitely further along
the road than that. This was a *modern* storehouse of
modern food. In fact they stored it better than we
have learned to do today."

He considered again; then he said, "I hope they
managed it better than we do; I hope they had solved
our problem of plenty. I hope they gave it away when
people were hungry, instead of holding out for a price,
or burning what they could not use. But perhaps this
was their basic problem too, the one that finally de-
feated them. Perhaps that was why their world came
to an end.

"I have often wondered what made that man on

guard come outside. Did he think someone was trying to steal his food? Or did he perhaps come out to give it away, and the world blew up in his face? If only I could have talked with him! If only we could know what the world was quarreling about!"

He mused, wandering off at a tangent; he said, "No doubt it was something utterly foolish, as it might be today. They had plenty of food; they had learned to harness power and growth; they could feed the world. Or perhaps they could only feed half the world, and the other half of the world had better eggs or caviar— or they were *thought* to have them. . . . But what appalling waste! They had learned to use the richest source of life, the sea; they had discovered the sea bed —the millions of years of sediment, the filtering down of dead fish, dead animals, dead men, dead weed; the compost heap of time itself."

Now he went off on a long, rambling aside; he said:

"The idea that we will starve because we will out-grow the earth's surface, that food only flourishes on land, is childish. What we produce on land is only a tiny spill-over from the true source of life—water. But if we must cling to these old-fashioned ideas, we can already go a long way towards conquering that problem. Sea water, distilled, can make a garden, a granary, out of all our modern deserts; the Sahara, the Kalahari, the center of Australia, the dry crusts of Texas and Arizona and Arabia. Yet if we truly want to learn from the past, we should study what the people of that early world accomplished. They made themselves another garden, on the sea bed itself."

Then he returned to what he called "the last quarrel," on which he must have thought most deeply of all. He said:

"Perhaps it did not concern food. These people had food in abundance. Perhaps, with all their technical advances, they remained as irrational as we are. Perhaps the fatal spark was pride. Or Helen of Troy. Or some crude insult at the Olympic Games. Or a miserable frontier dispute over ten square miles of swamp. Or the television rights to the moon. Or the color of a skin." For the first time he laughed. "Or the *thickness* of a skin. Perhaps it was a collision between the armadillo men and some softer race with delicate complexions and supple bodies, who thought themselves the tender elect. Perhaps they were only like us, after all; clever, accomplished, yet fundamentally greedy and suspicious.

"Perhaps their children were poisoned, as ours are, by adult ambition. Nearly all children are innocent and generous to start with; they could continue so, but they rarely do. You have only to watch refugee children in a Pestalozzi village—" I did not then know what he was talking about, though I do now "—to see this rule of innocence, this natural love. At the beginning they are all brothers. Then they catch an infection of hate, they breathe the corrupt air of battle, they grow claws, and most of them are lost forever."

He was silent for a long time after that; he looked exhausted to the point of death; I was afraid that we would hear little more save his disjointed wandering down the last pathway. But after he had rested and Mary had brought him warm milk and resettled his pillows, he rallied amazingly. He had much more to say, and I had never been so glad to listen. There were moments when I would have bought his life with my own.

He said, "But whatever the quarrel, we have the fact of destruction. Indeed, I believe that we have it on record, in our first and best history book. We cannot tell how much of the Bible is race memory, but I am sure it is an accurate picture of what has gone before. I am sure that our world was unaccountably born with knowledge of that remote past, that catastrophe. . . ." This was one of the few moments when he was watching my face instead of staring into the drab middle distance, and he must have found disbelief there, because he said energetically, "No, it is not too far-fetched! Consider the oldest tales of the beginning of the world. They speak of the earth vaporized, and gradually cooling; of swirling mists, invading seas. It is a perfect picture of the aftermath of an atomic explosion. And there are many other references to support the picture of a vast cataclysm.

"Take one of the simplest, the story of the Ark and the Flood. We read of a tidal wave lapping against high mountains, just *not* reaching the wretched survivors of some ruined plain. Don't forget, when the waters receded, those survivors would have to start all over again; however clever they might be, they would have nothing in the whole world to work with but water and a few balks of timber. . . . And Lot's wife, turning to look back at a city in flames, changed into a pillar of salt—instantly calcified, let us say, by unimaginable heat. Hiroshima also had its pillars of salt. After the fire-storm, there were human shapes fused into the very fabric of concrete buildings.

" ' The earth was without form, and void,' " said Shepherd. "I believe that was literally true. I believe it was shapeless, and empty, because these people had made it so. They learned how to blow themselves up, and then they went ahead and did it. *Perhaps it wasn't even the first time*. Perhaps it always happens. Perhaps we always go as far as we can in discovery, and then we go too far. Perhaps we have had Hiroshima before, many times. And then we made atomic faces at each other. And then we had the hydrogen bomb, and then we quarreled over Berlin, or Africa, or China, or food, or space. And then we did—whatever we're going to do next."

Interrupting for the first time, I said the first thing that came into my mind:

"God wouldn't allow it!"

The old man smiled, smoothing the worn blanket with a hand equally worn. "Ah, if I could believe that. . . . I must tell you that I have never believed, and I am not going to start now. It would be wrong. However much I want to. . . . If God is my kind of man—" I cannot begin to describe the wistful humility with which he said these strange words "—then He will forgive someone who denies Him to the end, even though that end terrifies him. Of course I am afraid of death, but I will not beg for mercy.

"For me, it is a matter of reason," he said. "It is so much more likely that the universe is ruled by chance than that God plans—or allows—our horrible mistakes and failures and accidents; the fire which burns a whole orphanage, the hurricane that destroys a city, the boy of ten who wastes away with leukemia. . . . Who, with power to prevent, could allow such things? Who could be so senseless and cruel? But if I am wrong, then *you* are wrong. God *would* allow us to destroy our world. He would have great patience. And great anger. And infinite belief. He would look down and say, 'If they annihilate themselves again, they deserve to. But perhaps this time. . . .' "

At that moment there was an interruption of the crudest possible sort. Without a word or a knock, the door sprang open, and Mrs. Cross advanced into the room.

She had not improved, nor softened; she was the same sort of person, plagued by anger and suspicion, plaguing us in return. She stood foursquare in the middle of the bedroom, looking from Mary to myself, looking last of all at the gaunt figure on the bed. Her voice was harsh as she said:

"What's going on around here?"

I got up and put myself between her and the bed, trying to mask and protect our charge. I said, "Nothing's going on. Mr. Shepherd is very ill, that's all. He mustn't be disturbed."

She bent, and peered around me; her eyes dwelt on the old man as if she were pricing his chances of life. Then she said:

"He's sick, he should be in hospital. That's what they're for. You planning to take him away?"

"Perhaps."

"He owes rent."

"It will be paid." I came nearer to her, trying to draw her towards the doorway again, out of earshot, anywhere; it was a shameful moment which I must somehow cancel out. "But I can't have him worried now."

"*You* can't!" Her voice exploded into sneering insult. "Who are you, for God's sake? Just tell me that! This is my house, and my room. It's a single room, not a convention hall!" She was looking at Mary now, with the utmost contempt. "You know what I mean, miss! It's time we straightened a few things up around here!"

Mary did not answer, did not even look in her direction; she also had half-risen and put her body between Mrs. Cross and the old man. I edged forward again, and said loudly:

"That's enough. Leave us alone."

"I'll decide what's enough!" said Mrs. Cross in a fresh fury. "This house is private. It's not a hospital. It's not a morgue, either!"

I cursed her; I hated her; I could have killed her then and there. To talk thus, in his hearing, as if he were not present, was iniquitous. Her sole purpose was to get him to die somewhere else. . . . I advanced again, until I was touching her and she had to fall back a pace. I said:

"He's staying here. And I'm staying here. And you're leaving now!"

She must have caught some desperation in my trembling voice, for she gave ground again, until she stood in the doorway. Her eyes darted around the room, as if she were memorizing the evidence for some vicious legal battle to come. She shouted, "We'll see about that!" and turned, and slammed the door behind her with shattering violence.

I looked immediately at the old man. The noise had shaken him, as it had shaken the whole rickety house; I could hear him gasping with shock. Though long subjected to Mrs. Cross, and ready to excuse and forgive her, he was not strong enough to withstand such barbarous thrusts. I foresaw then that this horrible invasion, topped off by the explosion of the slamming door, would be a mortal blow, that he would now begin to fail. The long shadows in the room seemed to grow deeper and darker as the scene changed for the one that must follow it.

But he could still joke about such things, in a very small way. Taking up his story once more, in a feeble whisper, he gave Mrs. Cross an oblique, gently satirical salute.

"You may not think so, at this precise moment, but we are not inevitably doomed to hate and destroy one another. . . . Of course we can balance the world on love and faith, any time we choose. We can make it the mirror of Paradise, if we want to. . . . Vaguely we do want to. But do we want to enough? Will we choose, in fact, or will we spit it all out in each other's faces?"

He began to ramble then, moving his head restlessly, speaking of a world-wide yearning for peace which had never been strong enough to overcome envy and suspicion. I had an idea that we had heard his last rational words; he was wasting before our eyes, and the word *waste* was a desolate one. Hungry to stay in touch with him, I began to ask random questions, anything I could think of to encourage him to answer.

"Why did you never go back?"

"I tried. . . ." His voice was intensely weary. "But first there was the war. . . . Then I tried for a long time to persuade people to believe my story. . . . I had very little money, and I was getting older. . . . Bone Lake was as near as I could come to it."

"Was it you who were in jail in America?"

"Oh yes." A wraith of a smile hung around his bloodless lips. "A man should go to jail for his beliefs at least once."

"But where is the ice mountain, exactly? Did you make a map of the area?" He did not answer me, but shook his head as if in doubt and remained staring into space. He was silent for so long that I prompted him, "Surely you remember a thing like that?"

Mary turned to frown at me, and whispered fiercely, "Don't ask questions! You must believe him!"

"You know that I do. It's just that I want—"

The old man himself interrupted me. "Yes, I made a map. I was trying to recall what happened to it. . . . I lost it during the war, with all else that I owned. . . . My clothes. . . . In a tanker, torpedoed. . . ."

He stopped again, and I urged him on, gently. "What about the other things, then?"

"Other things?"

"You said that you made up a parcel of food from the refrigerator and brought it back."

He nodded feebly. "Yes, that was so. . . . There was some meat, but it rotted to nothing as soon as it met the sun. . . . All the other things were lost—it was a very hard journey back—I had to leave so much behind, on the way. . . . I tried, but it was my life. . . . Of all I brought back, only one thing remained. . . . But I have it still."

I was conscious of an enormous, consuming excitement as I heard his last words; I could feel my very scalp prickling. If he had actual proof. . . . I waited while Mary wiped his forehead and neck, which were drenched with a sudden feverish sweat. Then I could no longer bear the silence and asked:

"What was it? What did you bring back?"

"Some of the concentrate," he answered readily, as if he had divined my overwhelming impatience. "I have kept it by me always, but I have never looked at it, nor shown it to anyone until now." He raised a trembling hand and pointed. "In the pocket of the rucksack."

My own hands were shaking so much that, after I reached up to the rucksack, I could scarcely undo the strap which secured the pocket flap. There was a hard, square object inside, and I drew it out carefully. It was a box of some kind, wrapped around and around with oiled silk which was frayed and cracked, as if it had lasted many years and been handled many times. I brought the package back to the light, and looked towards the old man. When he nodded, I slipped off a loop of tarred twine and started to unwind the wrapping.

Some of the layers had stuck to the ones beneath them and gave way grudgingly. But soon the roll of oiled silk fell to the floor with a dry, rustling sound. What I now held in my hands was an old tobacco tin, flat and hinged; the familiar face of the bearded sailor and the lifebelt were just visible on the scratched lid. I drew a deep breath, steadying my heart, and prized the lid open.

The tin was half full of a fronded green substance, loosely packed in strands; like a kind of long-fibered peat, but pale, the color of the ocean at dawn. When I bent down to it, a faint—a very faint—whiff of the sea reached me, a faraway echo of childhood beach-combing. Then, even as I stared in fascination, the packed strands began to lose their outline and to crumble away into ancient nothingness.

I wanted to shout, "I saw it! It saw it!" but already I could not be sure of what I had seen. Had it really been fronded seaweed? Had there really been tiny stems and buds and ferns, and the momentary scent of an ocean unspeakably old? What I was looking at now was a tin box with some loose, green, odorless dust at the bottom. It might have been anything. It might have been nothing. It might just have needed cleaning.

I said, foolishly, "It's gone," and looked towards the old man. His jaw had dropped, matching my own;

and on that note of ancient dissolution, he himself began to go.

He had sunk back on the pillow, deathly pale; his breathing grew hoarse. It seemed that he might slip into limbo at any moment, just as the fronded "concentrate" had disappeared before my eyes. Though close to mourning him already, I wished with all my heart that he could slip away as easily.

But there was to be one more interruption, perhaps the last of his life. A heavy knock on the door made me turn from where I had been standing, the dusty tobacco tin in my hand. I thought it was Mrs. Cross back again, and, between grief and wild disappointment, I was well prepared for her. But this time it was Sergeant Labelle.

10 CREDO

He advanced into the room like a heavy-stepping jailer, odiously confident, treading ground which became his own as soon as he set foot on it. Everything about him—the gun holster, the badged fur cap, the ruddy face and beefy torso—was immediately intolerable. He burst with crude life into a room already given over to death. I found it unbearable that he should trouble this pool at such a moment. Behind him was Mrs. Cross, backing up the invasion with her own brand of obscene interference.

Labelle took his time, looking at each one of us with a steady glare which might have been laid down in some secret-police manual. Only the glance he turned on the old man was brief, as if he knew enough about him already. Then he gave a hitch to his belt and said:

"What's going on?"

I was very ready to be the spokesman. "You can see, can't you?" I said. I had never yet spoken to a policeman in such a way, nor ever wanted to; in the circumstances it was a duty and a pleasure. "He's ill, and he doesn't want any visitors."

"Never mind what he wants," said Labelle, reacting predictably to my tone. "There's been a complaint." He jerked his head backwards towards Mrs. Cross. "He may be sick, but he doesn't have to be sick here. It disturbs the other tenants."

I pictured, swiftly enough, the other tenants, whom I had never seen. They did nothing to alter my resolve.

"He's not disturbing anyone," I answered, as roughly as I could. "You are disturbing him."

"Now just hold it there!" said Labelle with equal

roughness. "There's been a complaint, I've got to investigate it. If he's sick, he should be in hospital."

"He can't be moved."

"Why not?"

I did not answer immediately, but nodded towards the bed, compelling Labelle to follow my look. The old man's eyes were still closed, and his breathing was feather-light; it was the breathing which is the same for a baby or a dying man, the same for all humans at their beginning or their end. Then I said:

"You can see why not."

But Labelle was not tied to the protocol of the sick-room. "You mean he's dying?"

I said, as quietly as I could, "Yes, he's dying."

Mrs. Cross now joined the enemy advance. "That's what I told you," she said with a kind of venomous satisfaction. "The hospital is the place for him! I want the room!"

"He can't be moved."

"He can be moved any time I say so. I know my rights!"

Amazingly the old man stirred and opened his eyes. "We have no rights," he whispered. "Only responsibilities." But he was not answering Mrs. Cross; he was speaking to me, continuing what had gone before. "You saw it?" he went on anxiously. He was begging me to remember all that he had said and shown. "The seaweed concentrate?"

"Yes, I saw it."

"What's he talking about now?" asked Labelle impatiently.

Mrs. Cross came nearer to the bed. "Oh, he's always that way. I've had more trouble with this one. . . . Don't pay him any mind."

It was as if the old man were being forced out of life by its cruel pressures, its most sordid inhabitants. "For God's sake stop it!" I said in a furious whisper. "Can't you see. . . ."

I pushed her away from the bed, and sat down on it, opposite Mary. I was in agony lest Shepherd should die before he had said all that he could; now I wanted and willed him to stay alive. I knew that the wish was questionable, perhaps base; if the brutal people were killing him off, then I was not less brutal in delaying his death, at no cost to myself. But who could have resisted trying to keep him talking? What man would *not* have kept Nelson talking in *Victory's* shadowy cockpit, Lincoln mumbling amid bloodstained sheets, Christ alive on the Cross?

My weight upon the bed had recalled the old man to the world. He opened his eyes wide and looked directly at me. Though his voice was a deathly croak, it was clear enough for the living.

"Blessed are the meek," he whispered. "You know how that ends?"

"For they shall inherit the earth." It was incredibly moving to be able to make this response.

"The earth!" he repeated. "Not Heaven. The meek will take over the *earth*. . . . Remember that. . . . Make it happen in time."

His voice was so low that I had to bend to catch it. Mary was weeping; behind us Labelle and Mrs. Cross had fallen silent, subdued by the plainest fact on earth. The animals attendant on this wretched crib were docile at last.

Shepherd said, very slowly and painfully, "Don't forget that last man left alive. . . . He was not angry. . . . He was not really afraid. . . . He was— astonished."

After another long, gasping pause, he said, "Tell

them the story." Then his head fell aside on the pillow, and Death bandaged his eyes.

Neither of us could bear to stay in the room, which for us was already empty. As we went slowly down the stairs, I found that in my terrible hunger for life and hope I was holding Mary's hand. The death of one derelict had made, for a moment, two more.

From above us came vague footfalls, diminishing voices.

First, Labelle's: "Didn't have much, did he? . . . I could use that blanket."

And Mrs. Cross, indignant: "What about my rent?"

And Labelle: "What about my trouble? . . . Tell you what—I'll toss you for it."

Then we were clear of all this, and outside, in the crisp snow and bitter cold of what seemed more than ever God's fresh air.

That was three days ago. The poor burial is over, the mourners have fallen back from the grave side. Now it is necessary to believe, or not to believe.

Often I *know* that his story is true and that the old

man was left at Bone Lake to tell it to me. For a believer, there were clues all over the place. Yet I cannot always believe. So I must find out for myself.

It is still possible that I am the most gullible of
young men, even for a newspaper reporter, and that
this is just another northland legend, to be set alongside the Lost Valley and the vanished El Dorado. It is
possible that Shepherd was just a crazed old drunkard
who had only this fantasy to live on, and a tin of green
dust to back it up. It is possible that the Mad Trapper
had snared me, of all people (how easily one says and
thinks that), and that, in believing, I am simply taking
over from him as a second-generation crackpot.

Perhaps that is not important. Perhaps the actuality
does not matter, either. For, true or false, the idea beneath the story is valid. If it was hallucination, or
myth, it is still a good one, the best I ever heard.

So, during the sad confusion of the last few days, I
have believed most of it, and I want to believe all. This
burning need is what Shepherd somehow bequeathed
to me.

The *somehow* is still obscure, still a puzzle. They
say that one can be stabbed to death without feeling
the stroke. Perhaps one can be stabbed to life in the

same way. Maybe I will find that out as I go along. But if not, it is no great matter.

For everyone should have his quest, and I am lucky to have been given mine so early. If I can think of it as not less than a Holy Grail somewhere beneath the icecap, I may be luckiest of all.

In any case, I am off tomorrow, or the next day—as soon as Ed the pilot gets back and can be talked into taking a very long trip. If he will not, then someone else will. They must. For I *have* to find the great ice-box and the small, dark scaly man. I must put my hand into that—wound in the ice, and believe completely.

I will try to bring back some proof, so that others may believe too. Then we can spread news of it to all the world, to everyone—and that is you and I—who may be growing too proud or too greedy for the world's good.

Before it is too late, for all us brothers.